MW01268236

TWICE THE HEIST

Mark Cotton

This is a work of fiction. Names, characters, places and incidents either are the product of the author's imagination or are used fictitiously. Any resemblance to actual persons, living or dead, events or locales is entirely coincidental

LARGE PRINT EDITION

Copyright © 2018 Mark Cotton

All rights reserved.

ISBN: 1723483036
ISBN-13: 978-1723483035

To Cindy, for making life so much more than I ever imagined it could be.

PROLOGUE

Justin Ramey cursed and slammed his hand on the steering wheel. He knew immediately that turning off the highway and onto the dirt road was a bad mistake, one that might get him killed. For a few seconds he held onto a slim hope that the men in the black Ford Crown Victoria wouldn't follow on the rough graded caliche of the oil lease road. But, that hope disappeared when Justin saw the twin cones of the Crown Vic's headlights behind him, cutting through the cloud of dust he was leaving as he gunned the engine of the welding truck.

Justin didn't know who the men in the Crown Vic were, but the car itself had an ominous look and he didn't care to find out more about its occupants. He'd gotten a pretty good look at the car when it pulled up and parked a couple dozen feet away when he stopped at the Kwik-Pic in Van Horn for a mega-sized cup of iced Dr. Pepper and pack of cigarettes. The spotlight mounted just in front of the driver's door, the black wall tires, and plain black wheels with no hubcaps made it look like an undercover cop car. But, the windows were tinted darker than any police car, so Justin was pretty sure it wasn't the law when it parked and sat idling as he walked into the store. He had tried to look nonchalant as he made his purchases, aware that there might be someone watching his movements through the store's big plate glass windows.

The clerk was the same pretty blonde that he'd seen working the counter a couple of times before, but Justin was too distracted to think of a response when she made an obvious attempt to flirt with him.

Things hadn't gone quite right from the very beginning tonight, even before the black Crown Vic showed up. As he paid the cashier his focus was on getting back into the truck and making it back home to find out if he had screwed things up by not taking the time to find a pay phone and call somebody when the situation first started looking hinky.

It was a good job, even if Justin wasn't completely certain why he was being paid so much to drive a welding truck to a place three hours away and then turn around and drive a different welding truck back. All of the trips before this one had gone like clockwork. The other truck and its driver were always there waiting for him, inside a dirt lot surrounded by a chain-link fence topped with barbed wire. The other driver never spoke, just stood there waiting beside the other truck as Justin exited the identical truck that he had driven down from Andrews. Normally, they would do a quick exchange of keys and vehicles, and the other driver was out of the yard before Justin could even climb into the cab of the other welding truck. That always left the responsibility of closing and locking the gate to

Justin, which seemed fair since the other driver always got there first and had the gate unlocked and open.

The odd rendezvous routine was the only part of the job that was uncomfortable, made so mainly by the fact that Justin and the other driver never spoke. Justin had tried to strike up a conversation one time and the other driver just looked at him blankly, as if talking to another human being was a completely foreign concept. Justin figured the man, who had a Hispanic appearance, might not understand English, so he never tried talking to him again.

But, tonight's meeting had been different. Tonight, the other driver had someone else with him, the two of them waiting together when Justin drove in through the gate and parked beside the other truck.

They stood almost motionless next to the truck's front fender, and the driver seemed nervous and reluctant to look directly at Justin. The other man stood behind the driver watching, not speaking and only giving Justin a slight nod when their eyes met. After they exchanged keys, the driver stood where he was and waited as Justin got into the other welding truck and started it up. As he circled around the lot to leave, Justin glanced at the two men, who remained frozen and watching him. They were still standing there as he pulled out onto the street and drove away.

Justin wasn't supposed to stop at the convenience store that night, or anywhere else for that matter. That was one of the rules. But, after making the run a few times and being pretty certain that nobody would find out, he made it part of his routine to stop at the Kwik-Pik and grab something to eat and a package of smokes to kill the monotony of the long stretches of empty Texas highway between Van Horn and Mentone. But this time, when he had pulled out of the parking lot at the Kwik-Pik and glanced over at the outside rearview mirror of the welding truck to see that black Crown Vic fall in line behind him, Justin began to wish he'd followed the no-stopping rule a little closer.

But, it wasn't until a few blocks later, when he turned onto Farm-to-Market Road 2185, and the Crown Vic turned right along with him, that he really began to worry. Traffic on the old highway that ran past the Culberson County Airport was almost nonexistent at night since the interstate provided a much faster and more direct way to get anywhere east or west of Van Horn. The two-lane state road had narrow shoulders, twists and turns every few miles and a lower speed limit than I-10, which Justin would have preferred to take. But, regretting his forbidden stop at the Kwik-Pik he was determined to follow the rules as closely as possible for the rest of the night, which meant staying off of any main roads on the return trip.

FM 2185 was the first leg in a complicated and circuitous route home that Justin had driven each time he'd made the welding truck run, and one he'd committed to memory. He was familiar with the landmarks and knew which turns to take by heart. So, each time the route forked and the Crown Vic followed, it reinforced the notion that whoever was in the car was following him. He thought about using his cell phone to call somebody to ask them what to do, but that would mean letting his boss know that he'd broken another rule by bringing his cell phone along for the trip. No stops, no cell phones and always take the back roads on the way back. Well, at least he could say he'd followed one out of three of the rules.

The Crown Vic was running a steady quarter-mile behind him until they neared the town of Mentone, at which time the distance closed to less than a few car lengths. Justin felt some relief, sure whoever was in the car had simply gotten tired of trailing the welding truck and was getting positioned to pass. But, the car stayed on his tail all the way through Mentone, which was nothing more than a highway intersection with a few buildings scattered along six or eight short streets laid out in a grid pattern.

And then, once they were away from the lights of the little community, the Crown Vic pulled abreast of him on the two-lane road. Instead of passing, though, it matched Justin's speed and stayed there, as if they were on a four-lane interstate with no chance of meeting any oncoming traffic. Justin glanced over just as both blackened windows on the passenger side of the Crown Vic rolled down simultaneously. The glow of the car's interior lights allowed him to determine that there were four men in the car, two in front and two in back. He looked forward again, checking to make sure there were no headlights pointed in their direction, and when he looked back

over again, the two men on the
passenger side were each holding
guns, pointed directly at him.

Panic gripped him immediately
and his first impulse was to punch
the accelerator pedal and try to
pull ahead of the car. But the
welding truck was no match for the
Crown Vic, which easily maintained
its position as the needle on the
speedometer climbed higher and
Justin searched his mind for a way
out of the situation. The man in
the car's front seat was shouting
something, which would have been
impossible to hear at sixty-five
miles an hour, even if Justin's
window had been down. No
badges had been flashed, and
that's what the law always did
when they pulled up beside you on
TV, so Justin wasn't about to
comply with what the man was
yelling for him to do, even if he

could have understood it. But then the shooting started.

The first shot came from the shotgun the man in the backseat was holding, and the brunt of the blast made impact with the back corner of the truck's cab, just a few inches behind Justin's head, with stray pellets shattering the back window of the truck and creating a spider web of cracks in the driver's door window. The sound was deafening when the buckshot hit the cab, and startled Justin so badly that he almost lost control of the steering. He swiveled his head between the road and the shooter, trying to see through the crackled glass of the window to tell if another shot was coming so he would know when to duck. That's when he realized that the shotgun wasn't pointed at him, but at the area just behind the truck cab, where the large steel bottles of acetylene and oxygen were mounted in the custom-made welding bed. The shooter was taking aim as the man in the front seat continued to yell and gesture with his own gun, which looked like one of those military machine guns Justin had seen so many times when playing Nintendo, making it feel like he was trapped inside some kind of nightmare video game.

Justin didn't know enough about welding to know what might happen if the shooter happened to hit the gas bottles, but he wasn't about to find out. So, when the next shot hit and there was no ensuing explosion, Justin slammed on the truck's brakes and let the Crown Vic rocket ahead, then veered off the left side of the highway and onto a dirt oilfield lease road. He knew the area was dotted with well locations, each location marked by a solitary pumpjack, and all of them linked by a network of dirt roads constructed for the sole purpose of providing access to the wells. Leaving the highway was a desperate move, but he'd done it more on instinct than anything else.

And now, tearing down the rutted dirt road with the gas pedal floored and the Crown Vic looming larger in the rearview mirror, he strained to see beyond the reach of the welding truck's headlights, watching in case the road took a sudden turn to the left or right. There was no moon, and at the speed he was driving a half-second delay in response to a curve up ahead would mean the difference between keeping the truck on the road and sliding into a ditch and rolling over. But, it wasn't the fear of rolling the truck that scared him so much as the thought of what the men in the Crown Vic might do if they found him alive after a crash.

As it happened, he didn't have to wait long to find out. He negotiated the sudden curve in the lease road with no problem, but when he saw he'd turned into the short drive that led to the graded square of an isolated well location he knew there was nowhere else to go. He had driven right into a dead end. A slowly cycling pumpjack lay dead ahead in the center of the dirt square like a giant rocking horse. A pair rusted silver holding tanks stood to one side, and the flat, graded area was surrounded by sand dunes that would stop any vehicle within a few feet. He braked hard and turned the wheel of the truck, praying its tires wouldn't bite the rough caliche surface and cause it to flip. Before the truck stopped completely he was out the driver's door and scrambling towards the safety of the dunes. But, the Crown Vic was there immediately, its skidding stop adding to the cloud of dust created by the truck. As Justin ran blindly into the dark through the sand and mesquite, he heard angry voices shouting and the paralyzing metallic rattle of weapons being readied for firing.

CHAPTER ONE

sunday morning

Downtown Elmore, Texas was quiet and the sidewalks empty, as they always were on Sunday morning. None of the half-dozen antique stores that lined the streets surrounding the Starcher

County Courthouse would be open until Monday, and another half-dozen vacant buildings that had once seen life as dress shops or video rental stores, wouldn't open at all.   The courthouse itself was deserted for the weekend now that the county jail, formerly located in the basement, had been moved to a new facility north of town. Opposite one corner of the courthouse square, the Derrick Theater, a movie house where I spent Saturday afternoons as a kid, sat abandoned as it had been for at least fifteen years.   The tapered vertical facade, built to resemble an oil derrick, had once held enough neon tubing to rival a Las Vegas casino.   But the tubes were gone now, the victim of generations of late-night rock throwers and summertime hailstorms.

I parked my pickup in the parking lot of the Daze Gone Bye Antique Mall and walked to Lita's Little Mexico Restaurant on the opposite end of the block. As I walked, I studied the classic lines of the old theater building. I had always wanted to see it reopen, and at least once a month since moving back to Elmore I got the urge to track down the owners and attempt to rescue the building from them. There was another theater in Elmore, a four-screen complex housed in an ugly stucco box south of town, and it was barely breaking even, according to the local rumor mill. If the Derrick had been located in Austin or Dallas, it would have been re-opened long ago as a hip place to screen classic old black & white films alongside newer edgy art flicks, with craft beer and wine replacing the sugary off-brand colas that were dispensed in paper cups from a vending machine in the lobby when I was a kid.

The thick bundles of the Midland and Lubbock, Texas Sunday papers were lying on the sidewalk in front of Lita's entrance, alongside the much thinner Elmore Sentinel. I scooped them all up and continued on around to the side of the building. I stopped at a doorway halfway between the street and the alley. Black vinyl lettering on the door read: *Buddy Griffin, Private Investigations*. I had toyed with the idea of putting a big magnifying glass underneath the lettering but decided that would be a little bit over the top. As I put my key into the doorknob, I noticed a business card wedged between the door and the jamb. The elaborate seal of the Starcher County Sheriff decorated the visible end of the card. I pulled it out and read the handwritten note on the back: *Buddy, call me when you get in. We need to talk.*

It was Norris Jackson's business card. Norris had gone to work as a Sheriff's deputy in Starcher County a couple of decades earlier, shortly after I joined the Austin Police Department. Norris stuck with it and eventually ran for the office of Sheriff and got elected. Down in Austin, I stuck with the job too, working my way through the APD until I reached the Homicide Division, where I stayed until I got old enough to take early retirement. Norris was a few years younger than me, but we had a lot in common. And, unlike some of the guys with the local Elmore Police Department, he didn't treat me like I had deserted the law and crossed over to the other side just because I became a private eye.

My office was located next door to Lita's Little Mexico Restaurant. The truth was, it was actually *inside* Lita's building, which came in quite handy when I got hungry. The restaurant was owned and operated by Manuelita and Pete Rascon, having been opened in the 1960's by Manuelita's parents. Her father named it after Manuelita when she was still a little girl and handed the place over to her when she was old enough to run it. When the business migration out of downtown Elmore began to affect their revenue, Lita's husband Pete came up with the idea of partitioning off one of the unused dining rooms and renting out office space. Apparently, nobody ever pointed out to Pete that there were half a dozen vacant buildings within a stone's throw of Lita's front door. Office space in downtown Elmore was not in short supply. But, I'd always loved the food at Lita's, so when I moved back to town and was looking for a place to park my answering machine, drink coffee and read my newspapers each morning, I decided to become the Rascon's first tenant. Pete Rascon tried to be helpful by sending new clients my way, but none of them had turned out to be *paying* clients yet. However, helping them out had given me something to do while I waited for more business to develop.

I pushed open the door and glanced around as I came in, walked across the floor and opened a second door, which led from my office into the restaurant. The restaurant was dark and quiet, the chairs still stacked on the tables.

Scanning the inside of the restaurant each morning was part of my routine. Old cop habit. It wouldn't do much for my reputation as an investigator if somebody came in later and discovered a burglary had taken place right under my nose.

One of the drawbacks of having an office inside a Mexican restaurant was the fact that if I spent much time there I ended up smelling like whatever the special was that day. It was often distracting to my underworld sources. It's hard to remember who shot who over which bad drug deal when your stomach is focused on the scent of cheese enchiladas wafting through the air. Of course, the location had its advantages too. While some of the upper middle class, law abiding types of Elmore had abandoned downtown completely for the new restaurants located out near the Wal-Mart Supercenter, most of the people who were useful to me in my work still ended up eating at Lita's sooner or later.

The smell of the Saturday night fish special was still pretty strong in my office, and the weather outside was nice, so I propped open the door to the street with one of two guest chairs from in front of my desk. I filled the coffeemaker and sat down at the desk to scan the papers. I subscribe to the Midland paper because the cities of Midland and Odessa are less than an hour away. And, I read the Lubbock paper because my only daughter, Adrienne is attending Texas Tech University Medical School there. Elmore's newspaper is struggling to stay in business, so I feel an obligation to subscribe, even though the best thing the paper has going for it are lots of pictures of local residents attending social functions.

Before I could get settled in and take the plastic bags off of the newspapers, I heard the sound of a car rounding the corner and looked up to see Norris Jackson's cruiser pull to the curb.

"Bad timing," I said, as his six-foot-five silhouette filled the doorway. "Coffee's not ready yet. And there aren't any donuts today."

"Well, shit. Guess my instincts are failing me," he said, collapsing into the guest chair in front of the desk and wrinkling up his nose. "Smells like fried fish in here."

"You been circling the block, waiting for me to show up?" I asked.

He shook his head once, cutting our traditional verbal jousting short.

"You hear about Benny Shanks?" he asked.

Shanks was a local bar owner who also ran a pawn shop and owned most of the vending and video game machines in the county. His legal name was Benjamin Schankowitz but was known to everybody around Elmore as Benny Shanks. He was a long-time member of a loosely organized crime group that controlled the gambling and dope franchises around west Texas and eastern New Mexico.

"What's he doing now?" I answered. "Bringing those hookers from Amarillo back down here?"

Norris laughed.

"I had completely forgotten about that little operation. No, Benny won't be running any more hookers around these parts, or anywhere else for that matter. He cashed in his chips early this morning."

"Benny's dead?" I asked.

"Uh-huh. One of the Elmore PD cruisers found him shot to death in that big old Eldorado of his over on Avenue B. He took one behind his left ear. Made a helluva mess."

"Benny Shanks," I said. "Are you surprised?"

"Naw, not really, I guess. Benny had a lot of enemies. I'm really surprised he made it this long before it caught up with him."

"I wonder what he was doing on Avenue B," I said.

"That's a real good question. Up to no good, I'd wager. Adams will probably put Clemmer on it. He's the only one didn't end up covered in shit from that fiasco out at A.J.'s".

Dave Adams was the Elmore Chief of Police and Bob Clemmer was a veteran detective with the Elmore PD. Adams had been up to his ass in controversy since a questionable shooting at A.J.'s Lounge eight months earlier. A young black man had gone to the lounge looking for the man who'd stolen his girlfriend. When he found him, a fight broke out and half of the Elmore Police Department descended on the lounge like they were taking down an international terrorist. When it was all over, two of the bar patrons were dead and three more had gunshot wounds. All of the victims were black and a majority of the police who responded to the call had been white. Three weeks later, the ACLU and the Black Lives Matter movement got involved, and the incident and its aftermath had been on the front page of the Elmore Sentinel ever since.

Cleveland Campbell, a well-known African American businessman from Austin had taken a personal interest in the case and had been making frequent trips to Elmore to visit with leaders of the local black community. It may have been no coincidence that Campbell was currently making a run for the Texas House of Representatives.

I picked Norris' business card up off the desk and waved it at him.

"Was this about Benny?"

"Yeah. I thought I'd talk to you to see if you knew anything that might point to who did it."

"I thought the city guys were handling it."

"They are. I'm just thinking ahead in case the Sheriff's Office gets pulled in. Some of Benny's more unorthodox business interests extended beyond the city limits, you know. I was wondering if his associates in Odessa got pissed off at him over something. And you being so tight with Sandy Doyle and all."

Sandy Doyle was a player in organized crime in West Texas and had been for decades. I'd had a run-in with Sandy while working on another case a few months earlier and Norris had helped me out.

"The City cops will probably have trouble getting anywhere on a shooting that took place in a black neighborhood, given the current political climate," I said.

"Well yeah, there is that too," he conceded. "Word on the street is that Cleve Campbell isn't going to let up on the thing at A.J.'s until the cops involved are behind bars."

"Or, until Cleve gets himself elected to the state legislature," I said.

"Whichever comes first I guess," he answered with a shrug, walking over to check on the coffee. "You really don't have any donuts?"

"Nope," I said. "The donut shop doesn't even open on Sunday."

"Bunch of religious nuts, you ask me."

"Maybe I could go down the street to the church and borrow a communion wafer for you," I said.

"No, that's okay. Lord, it really does smell like fried fish in here. How do you ever get any work done?"

"Persistence, instinct and reasoning, along with pride, desire and hustle," I said. "Besides, the heavenly aroma of Mexican food will replace the fishy smell within a few hours."

"You really don't have anything to contribute on Benny?" he asked.

"Sorry, Norris. But I'll keep an ear open. What do you think happened?"

He walked to the open doorway and surveyed the empty street.

"Well, obviously Benny pissed somebody off, but I don't think it was anybody from Odessa. I've heard that Benny was doing some business with somebody local. Moving some dope. Maybe three or four somebody's. Big shipments."

"Anybody I know?"

"Nobody I can talk about yet. I want to see if you come up with the same names I've been running into."

"Can't just give me a hint?" I asked.

Norris moved to the coffeemaker and took two Styrofoam cups from a plastic bag and filled them with coffee. He placed one on the desk in front of me.

"You know," he said. "There are a lot of resourceful people around town. You grew up here, so you've seen activity in the oilfield go up and down like a yo-yo your whole life. When business is good, there's a new oilfield service company on every block. And, when things slow down again, most of those companies get shaken out and file bankruptcy. The survivors are usually the ones who don't throw money around when times are good; the ones who know things can turn around and go south in a heartbeat."

"And, the others?"

"The others?" he asked.

"The others who survive," I said. "You said the ones who *usually* survive are the most frugal."

"Did I use the word frugal?" he asked.

"I doubt that you've ever used that word. I was paraphrasing. You think somebody in the oil business is branching out into other enterprises?"

"I'm just repeating rumors," he said. "I don't have any facts to support anything."

"Who needs facts?" I said. "They just complicate matters."

Norris was staring out the doorway at something in the distance as he sipped his coffee.

"Why are you really so interested in who dropped Benny?" I asked. "There's something else, isn't there?"

He turned and looked at me steadily for a few seconds before answering.

"Buddy, did you ever--".

He stopped in mid-sentence, looked down and shook his head.

"Just let me know if you hear

anything about Benny. And, keep it on the QT if you don't mind. I don't want to piss off anybody at City Hall."

Norris' radio squawked and he had to cut our visit short to tend to some business at the other end of the county.

Something was bothering Norris, and it seemed to have something to do with Shanks' murder, but I could tell he wasn't ready to talk to me about it yet, so I hadn't pushed.

I sipped my coffee and watched the morning inactivity outside my doorway while I thought about the untimely, yet inevitable, passing of Benny Shanks.

During my high school years, Benny was known as a reliable source of alcohol for underage drinkers. And, since it was hard to maintain your reputation as a popular athlete at Elmore High unless you drank a beer now and then, I'd gotten to know Benny. I probably even received special attention since my performance on the football field had a direct impact on his gambling winnings. Benny and I ran into each other again when I moved back to Elmore, opened up my PI business and started working cases. Angie and I enjoyed having dinner and a drink at Benny's bar, The Pumpjack Club, every now and then. Benny was a genuine local character, and one who had played an important part in Elmore's local history, albeit a part that sometimes showed up on the police blotter.

Norris' idea that Benny had found an otherwise legitimate local businessman to partner up with wasn't so far-fetched. Most of the players in the local oil business had come of age in an era when skirting the law to get the job done wasn't an uncommon practice. And, most local oil men were in oil partnerships with a wide range of people. In the oil business, it's common for several investors to share the risk and potential reward of drilling and developing an oil well. My father had been in numerous partnerships over the years, and he and my mother had lived comfortably on oil and gas royalty checks after he retired.

The practice of forming partnerships to share the risk tended to spill over into other types of local business ventures too. Many of the local restaurants and retail operations were started by people in the oilfield with a desire to branch out and diversify their interests.

Maybe Norris was right. Maybe

the slowdown in the oil patch, and the resulting dip in the local economy, had driven some of the more *resourceful*, as Norris had put it, to invest in a drug distribution partnership with Benny.

Only time would tell.

CHAPTER TWO
wash-o-mat

After Norris left, I spent a few minutes reading the Sunday papers and enjoying the quiet. Lita's didn't open until noon and was one of the few downtown businesses that opened at all on Sunday, so the only sounds were from the odd car passing by now and then. When I got up to refresh my coffee, I looked out and saw Elmore's only street person shuffling toward my doorway pushing the ancient Piggly Wiggly shopping cart that held his most important possessions. When he looked up and saw me he quickly shifted his eyes away but gave a disciplined two-fingered Cub Scout salute, which I returned.

I took my coffee back to my desk and he appeared in the doorway a few seconds later.

"Good morning, Cuatro," I said. "You doing okay today?"

"Morning, morning, morning, morning," he said, his eyes looking everywhere but directly at me.

"There's some coffee left there if you want some," I said.

He gave a quick smile that was more like a wince and started toward the coffee pot.

"Best-part, best-part, best-part, best-part" he said, adding instant creamer and an unbearable amount of sugar to the cup he had just poured.

"Is it washday today?" I asked.

"Wishy-washy, wishy-washy, wishy-washy, wishy-washy," he said in response.

"Let me lock up here and we'll walk on down there," I said, picking up the newspaper sections I hadn't read yet.

We stepped outside and I locked up before we walked across the street, past the courthouse and across another street to the Spin-Cycle Wash-o-Mat, a coin-operated laundromat that was closed on Sundays. I unlocked the front door and turned on the lights, then held the door open as Cuatro rolled his shopping cart inside.

"Wash-dry, wash-dry, wash-dry, wash-dry," he said as he opened one of the washer doors and began pulling dirty clothes from a black trash bag inside the shopping cart.

The laundromat, and the fact that

it was closed on Sundays, was the reason I had come to know Cuatro. Not long after I moved back to Elmore I was asked if I wanted to serve on the board of the local Crimestoppers organization since I had a background in law enforcement. At one of the meetings, the owner of Spin-Cycle complained that his building had been broken into three times, although nothing was ever taken and no damage was done. Each of the break-ins had occurred sometime between Saturday at midnight, when the laundromat was locked up, and six in the morning on Monday, when it reopened.

A few weeks later the laundromat owner came to see me. The weekend burglar had been caught, but the owner wanted my advice about whether or not to press charges. The police had found the culprit inside the laundromat on a Sunday afternoon, wearing only his underwear while his other clothes were being tumbled dry in one of Spin-Cycle's machines. The police had trouble getting the burglar to answer questions or tell them his name and were holding him until something could be figured out. I agreed to go to the police station with the laundromat owner to help him decide what course of action to take.

As he was leading me back to the cell where the burglar was being held, the jailer seemed genuinely frustrated by the behavior of his inmate.

"I'll be damned if I can figure out what he's talking about half the time," he said. "He isn't violent, and seems to be friendly enough, but most of what he says is just gibberish."

"And, he won't tell you his name?" I asked.

"Nope. Now the patrol guys tell me he's been around here for years, they all call him Cuatro, but nobody seems to remember how they learned that much."

"Hi Cuatro," I said, standing outside the bars of the holding cell. "Mind if we talk for a few minutes?"

"Talk, talk, talk, talk," he answered.

"Do you know why you're in here?" I asked.

"Cop, cop, cop, cop," he said. I was beginning to understand how Cuatro had gotten his street name.

"Listen, Cuatro. I know you've been breaking into the laundromat to do your laundry when there's nobody there. We need to figure out a better way for you to do your laundry so the police will leave you alone."

"Clean, clean, clean, clean," he said softly, examining a cut in the rubber of one of his grimy running shoes.

"Can you do your laundry when the laundromat is open?" I asked.

"People, people, people, people," he said, shaking his head.

"Okay," I said. "We'll figure out something. Private, private, private, private."

He looked up and smiled like he'd finally found someone he could understand, and I felt we made a connection.

"Four times?" the jailer asked, after I pointed out Cuatro repeated everything four times and that was likely the source of his nickname. "I guess I hadn't even noticed."

I explained to the owner of the laundromat that Cuatro had only broken in so that he could use the coin-operated machines at a time when there weren't so many other patrons around. He decided not to press charges and we worked out an arrangement where I would unlock the doors on Sunday, sit with Cuatro while he did his clothes, and then lock the place back up when we were finished.

I was glad the owner agreed to my proposal. It would have been so much easier for him to refuse to drop the charges and to have Cuatro barred from ever setting foot inside his place again. But, I've found over the years that even the coldest of personalities can have the ability to dredge up some compassion for a fellow human being if they come to understand that person's situation more fully.

With the laundry problem settled, I found a place for Cuatro to live, in an old unused parsonage building behind the Lutheran Church, although he preferred spending his time outside except during the coldest nights in the winter.

During most of our laundry sessions, Cuatro was generally upbeat and repeating words and phrases left and right. But, today he had been unusually quiet, and I could see something was bothering him. He was just finishing up folding, sorting, and stowing his laundry in his grocery cart as I finished the last of my newspaper. He quietly rolled outside and waited as I turned out the lights and locked up again.

This was normally the point where Cuatro would turn to me and say "Fine and dandy, fine and dandy, fine and dandy, fine and dandy," and we would part company. Always the same line, and he would always walk off in the opposite direction of my office.

But, when I turned around this time, he was just looking down at the cracked sidewalk between us. He glanced up at me a couple of times and finally looked directly at me, which is something Cuatro had never done before.

"Something wrong?" I asked.

"Big-fight, big-fight, big-fight, big fight," he said, nodding.

He stared at me, waiting for a response.

"I'm not following you. Did you get in some kind of fight?"

He shook his head.

"Boom, boom, boom, boom!" he said, his eyes wide.

"Somebody else got in a fight?"

He nodded vigorously. "Bad, bad, bad, bad!"

Then he quickly began digging through the stuff that was

crammed in his shopping cart. He
stopped and looked around and
then raised his hand and made a
writing motion, then made a fist
and pumped his thumb like he was
holding a ballpoint pen and pointed
to my breast pocket.

I pulled a small notepad out of my
pocket and held it out with my
ballpoint pen. He took the pen but
ignored the offered pad. He bent
over his cart and used the ballpoint
to fish out a large convenience
store drink cup. He held it out to
me, balanced on the ballpoint pen.
I reached to take it off the pen, but
he drew it back.

"Careful, careful, careful, careful,"
he said.

Then, he cautiously turned the
pen around so I could take the
pen, with the cup balanced on it,
without touching the cup.

"Evidence, evidence, evidence,

evidence," he said quietly, before turning away and rolling his cart off down the sidewalk.

I stood there watching him for a few seconds before walking back to my office with the upended drink cup still balanced on my ballpoint pen. I didn't know quite what to make of what had just happened, but my relationship with Cuatro often tended to have confusing interludes of communication, so it really wasn't that unusual. Inside my office, I started to dump the dirty cup in the trash, but on a hunch decided to set it on top of a filing cabinet while I thought about why it might be so important to Cuatro.

With the cup sitting upright, I could see the inside had dried traces of a sticky blue residue from whatever sweet concoction the cup had originally contained. In my time with Cuatro at the Wash-O-Mat, and on our monthly trips to the recycling center to turn in the cans he collected, I had never seen him drink anything but water. So, I was pretty sure the cup wasn't something he bought for himself. The outside of the cup was decorated in a colorful design using psychedelic letters to spell out "Texas Brain Freeze" and included the logo of Big Mama's Convenience Stores. There wasn't a Big Mama's store in Elmore, but there were locations in nearby towns, and all across Texas.

It wasn't all that unusual to see a discarded cup from a Big Mama's store on the streets of Elmore, but for some reason Cuatro thought this particular one was important enough to give to me and to avoid handling directly. And, his last words referring to the cup as "evidence" piqued my curiosity even further.

Using an LED flashlight, I carefully examined the inside and outside of the cup.   On the outside, hidden among the shapes and colors that made up the intricate Texas Brain Freeze design, I thought I could make out some tiny dark-colored dots that weren't part of the printing.   And, I found an even smaller dark red dot on the white inside lip of the cup.   I thought about putting the cup in a plastic bag and walking it down to the Elmore Police Department building, in case it really was evidence of some kind of crime.   But, it was Sunday, and even though the Elmore PD operated round the clock it was still easier to talk to people there during business hours on a weekday.   It would have to wait.

CHAPTER THREE
loose lips

My parents lived in Elmore until dying within months of each other, not long before I retired from the Homicide Division of the Austin Police Department. They were both healthy and vigorous up until they were in their eighties. Mother died first, and then Dad lost interest in continuing on without her. He told me that after being with my mother since they were teenagers it felt like part of him just wasn't there anymore.

They had named me executor of their estate since I was the only one of their three boys who still lived reasonably close. I tried handling things from Austin, but it just didn't work out, so I began making frequent trips back to Elmore trying to wrap things up, sell my parents' place and weigh my options for life after being a cop for more than two decades. Then, while I was in town on a visit, my high school sweetheart's husband was murdered and I got involved in the investigation as a favor to her. I was able to find out what led up to the murder and, with some help from Norris Jackson, resolve a dangerous situation before anyone else was killed.

Norris convinced me there was a need for a private investigator in the area, so I half-heartedly set up shop in Elmore. I figured I would return to Austin as soon as I got the estate settled, but the PI practice would provide enough activity to keep me out of trouble in the meantime. Then, a problem with an easement delayed the sale of my parents' house and oil prices took a nosedive, which made it a bad time to try to sell my parents' oil royalty interests. My father's attorney had introduced me to one of his associates, an attractive female oil and gas specialist, and my interest in returning to Austin began to fade. The attorney's name was Angie Robbins, and I began to have trouble concentrating on business any time she was around. Angie advised me to sit on the oil royalties until prices stabilized, but I kept manufacturing reasons why we needed to get together to discuss the issue further.

Luckily, she seemed to be just as interested in me as I was in her and we began seeing each other on a regular basis. We settled into a routine of spending Sunday afternoon at the movies, followed by dinner out. Sometimes we drove down to Midland or Odessa for the expanded choice of theaters and restaurants. Today, Angie was hosting a Sunday afternoon cookout at her place to try out a new barbecue grill I had helped her select. I would be doing the cooking, which was only right since all of the guests would be people I had introduced her to since we'd started dating.

As I parked and walked up the walk to Angie's front door, I could hear the screams of a group of kids playing in the yard next door. The day was warm, and it was one of those rare spring days in West Texas when the air wasn't filled with red dust from fifty-mile-an-hour winds. Angie answered the door looking better than most women could with half a day of preparation. But, I knew from experience that she had probably jumped in the shower less than an hour before.

"Did you hear about Benny Shanks?" she asked, after a quick kiss.

"You mean he finally came out of the closet?"

She jabbed me in the ribs. "You already know, dammit! I've got all these inside sources and they never do me any good. You always get the scoop on me."

"Lawyers are never the first to find out when somebody gets murdered. You know that," I said.

"John says Chief Adams will

probably call a big press conference and blow this thing up to take the heat off the shootings at A.J.'s."

John was John Donnelly, Angie's boss and my father's attorney for decades.

"Does John have any idea who went after Benny?" I asked as I followed her into the kitchen where she was organizing the food.

"No. He said Chief Adams himself probably hired somebody to do it, you know, to divert attention from the fact that his police department's been getting beat up in the news lately."

"Wouldn't be a bad strategy," I said. "How much do you know about Benny?"

She shrugged. "Not a lot besides the fact that he owned The Pumpjack Club, B & M Vending and Benny's Pawn and Loan. Oh, and I almost forgot about Field Hands, that temporary employment service. Of course, I've also heard all the rumors that he was a bookie and probably a drug dealer."

"Nothing about who he might be in bed with?" I asked.

"Not really, why?" she said, turning her attention to a Ziploc bag of roasted green chiles she was defrosting in the microwave.

"Norris seems to think Benny had a local partner, maybe a businessman who decided to make an investment in the drug trade."

"Did he mention anyone in particular?" she asked.

"No, but I think he's got some ideas. He just wants to see if I come up with the same names working on my own."

"Since when does the county sheriff hire a private detective to help with an investigation?"

"Oh, he's not. It's nothing official, just a couple of old farts speculating about what might have happened. You know how cops and ex-cops are. Norris' department isn't even involved in the case yet. He just thinks it might spillover to the County at some point."

"Well, if you're going to look into it you probably want to tread lightly," she said, concentrating on the chiles. "This is a small town and news travels pretty fast. It sounds like this is the type of thing that could piss all the wrong people off."

"Piss people off? Who, me? Seriously, do you think I care if I piss off a few of the movers and shakers around here?"

"I guess not," she said with a shrug. "Would you mind slicing this onion for me? A big strong man like you can probably do it without crying."

I found a cutting board underneath the cabinet and a large Henckels knife in a drawer and began making nice even slices, perfect for hamburgers. After a few seconds of silence, I realized the temperature in the room had dropped ten degrees. My curiosity about the possible involvement of a local businessman in Benny Shanks' drug operation bothered Angie, and I couldn't understand why. I should have taken her silence as a signal to drop the subject, but I wouldn't be a very good investigator if I let good judgment overrule my curiosity.

"You already know who it is, don't you?" I asked.

"No, I don't," she answered, a bit too quickly. "I just know that if you go around asking people you're liable to hear anything about anybody. And, you've still got to live in this town when it's all over. So, do I."

I had finished with the onion and worked at arranging the slices on a big platter alongside slices of cheese and other optional additions for the burgers. It gave me a few seconds to think about what I was going to say next, lest I wander deeper into the minefield I found myself standing in.

"Is it going to be a problem for us if I look into this? Are you worried I might step on the toes of some of Donnelly's clients?"

"What do you mean?" she asked.

"The Donnelly Firm is the white glove law outfit around here," I said. "Where else would a smart, successful businessman go, especially a businessman that dabbles in illegal drugs and needs the best legal representation money can buy?"

"I don't know what you're talking about.   Can you hand me one of those forks in that drawer?"

"That's it, isn't it?" I asked. "You think it might be one of your clients, don't you?

She stopped what she was doing and looked at me.   "You know I can't discuss this with you. Ethically, I'm not even supposed to acknowledge if someone is or isn't a client."

"Well, ethically you shouldn't have allowed me to do what I did night before last, but you did."

"Now you're confusing ethics and morals, Mr. Griffin.   Good job on the onion, by the way."

"Thank you.   Okay, if you won't dish about your clients maybe we'll have to change the subject.   Let's see, did you have fun in Midland?"

Angie and two of her friends had spent Saturday hitting the stores in the nearby city.

"We did," she said, the tension in her voice dissipating. "We didn't get back until late last night. I'll show you what I got if we have time before everybody gets here. What did you do yesterday?"

"McMurtry and I spent most of the morning working in the yard, and then we napped in front of the TV together."

McMurtry was one of the cats living behind my parents' place, where I'd been living since moving back to town. Of the half dozen or so in residence at any given time, McMurtry was by far the friendliest of the bunch, the rest being feral.

The doorbell rang and Angie sent me to answer it while she stayed in the kitchen. Ray and Melba Garcia were the first to arrive with a

Crockpot full of chile con queso and several bags of locally-made tortilla chips. Melba once spent half an hour lecturing me about buying mass-produced tortilla chips and the impact it had on the local economy. Ray and I had been friends since high school and had kept in close touch over the years.

As I was closing the door after letting Ray and Melba in, I noticed Ham Burnett's ancient Chrysler slowly rolling up the street. I waved and he parked at the curb and climbed out carrying a large glass jar filled with sun tea. Ham was a widower, and he was twenty years older than anyone else in the group. Ray and I had gone to school with Ham's son, but he had died of a drug overdose a few years earlier. I had met Ham while working a case and we'd found that we enjoyed each other's company.

Once, Angie had gently suggested that I might be trying to make up for time missed with my own father when he was older, and I couldn't argue with her on that.

I took Ham's jar of sun tea and ushered him back to the kitchen, where Angie, Melba and Ray were already deep into a discussion of the fine points of making guacamole dip. Angie put me to work peeling avocados and combining their flesh in a bowl while she answered the door. The voices of Jake Sutton, Sid Fuller and Louis Rogers, our remaining guests, joined the cacophony in the kitchen. Jake, Sid and Louis were all retired and were as inseparable as Siamese triplets. They spent at least a couple of hours most mornings drinking coffee at Lita's, where a waitress had dubbed them the Three Amigos, a name they were proud to repeat every chance they got.

With the dips made, drinks dispensed and food ready to put on the grill, we moved outside. There were at least four different conversations going at once, but they all came to a stop when Ray Garcia mentioned Benny Shanks' shooting.

"I heard he got shot in the back of the head," Ray said. "Blew his brains all over the dashboard. Excuse me ladies."

"Ray!" Melba said. "My God. And you wonder why I never take you out in public."

"I thought you didn't take him out in public because of how he looks," Sid said.

"It just won't be the same without old Benny around," Jake said. "Who's gonna take bets on the Superbowl next year?"

"I remember when we were in high school Benny used to sell a bunch of us guys beer," Ray said. "I went in The Pumpjack Club the other day and some of the same guys he used to sell beer to when we were in high school were sitting there at the bar, still buying beer from him today. The man knew how to develop and maintain a loyal customer base."

"That's for sure," Jake said. "If you ever placed a bet with Benny, he could always remember who you bet on and would give you a call when your team was playing again."

"Well, he may have been a good old boy and friendly as all get-out," Louis said. "But I've also heard that he was responsible for most of the drugs that come into town."

"There's definitely some truth to that," Ray said. "But, he's not the only player in the game. I think you'd be surprised at some of the folks who've got a finger in that pie."

"Anybody you care to mention?" Sid asked.

Ray looked at Melba, who was shaking her head, and then reached up and made a motion like he was zipping his lips, turning a key in a lock and throwing the key away. It was one of the few times I'd ever seen Ray hesitate to say what was on his mind or volunteer his opinion on a controversial subject.

"Oh, come on now," Sid said. "We're all grown-ups here. And, it's not like there haven't been local big-wigs caught with their pants down before. Are any of you old enough to remember that bootlegging scandal way back?"

"When was that?" Melba asked.

"I don't think I ever heard about it."

"Oh, geez," Sid said. "It was back in the sixties, I think. Before you could buy booze in Starcher County. A couple of city councilmen were involved in sneaking cases of liquor up from Odessa. There was a group trying to get it on the ballot to vote Starcher County to go wet and these two guys fought it tooth and nail. Turns out they had a vested interest in keeping the county dry."

"I remember that," Ham said with a chuckle. "Caused a pretty big stink when it all came out, but it was common knowledge that you could buy all the booze you wanted around here if you just knew who to call. They'd deliver it right to you, cash on delivery. It all came out in the newspaper. Back then, the locals who were making the most noise about the evils of alcohol were the same folks paying regular visits to that first Pinkie's Liquor Store you come to on the highway into Odessa."

"And all the country club hotshots drinking that illegal booze back in the sixties were the same type of people doing lines of cocaine in the back rooms during the eighties," Sid said.

"And, the cops were too scared to shut down any of those nose-candy parties back then," Jake said. "Afraid they might be busting somebody on the city council."

"Are we saying Benny had some help from some well-known parties when he was doing his drug dealing?" Sid asked. "Come on, spill it somebody. I lost all my good sources for local gossip when I retired."

"Well, I can tell you Dallas Jenkins

flies his private plane down to Mexico at least once a month, supposedly to go fishing," Ray said.

I glanced at Angie in time to see a flash of anger in her eyes that quickly disappeared. She noticed me watching and smiled but she couldn't hide her irritation.

"Raymond, I need your help in the kitchen," Melba barked, grabbing Ray's arm and marching him toward the back door.

"Uh-oh," Sid said, laughing. "Just couldn't keep that lip zipped, could you?"

The topic of conversation veered towards professional football and all speculation about who might or might not be involved in drug trafficking was left behind for the rest of the evening. A cold front hit shortly after we finished eating. The wind quickly picked up, in typical west Texas fashion, dropping the temperature, filling the air with dust and blowing loose napkins, paper plates and cups around the patio. The sudden change in the weather moved the party inside, where it began to wind down.

Within a few minutes, everyone left except for Ray and Melba, who stayed behind to help clean up. Angie was still playing the gracious hostess, but I could tell she was bothered about Ray's earlier comment implying that Dallas Jenkins might be involved in something illegal. What happened next only escalated the tension.

I was bringing in a few remaining items from the back patio, and while I had the back door opened, Ray opened the front door while using both hands to carry Melba's crock pot out to their car. A gust of wind from the open back door swept right through the house and caused the front door to slam shut with such force that it sent an antique vase on a table next to the door toppling to the floor, where it shattered. As Angie and Melba rushed out of the kitchen to see what happened they saw Ray standing by the door, the crock pot in his hands desperately trying to apologize for something that really wasn't his fault.

Angie put on her best face, telling Ray and Melba not to worry about it, when it was easy to see the incident had upset her even further. Conversation was stilted and forced for the next few minutes until Ray and Melba decided it was best to leave, repeating offers to pay for the broken vase to Angie's refusal to even consider it.

"Ray never has been able to keep his mouth shut and mind his own business," I said as we stood in the front doorway watching their car pull away from the curb.

"I just don't understand how the man stays in business," Angie said, openly showing the anger she was still feeling. "Why would somebody entrust their confidential financial information to somebody who's such a gossip?"

"I'm sure he was only repeating what's being said about Dallas Jenkins by lots of other people in town," I ventured as I tried to help her pick up the pieces of the vase.

"Well, that's why they call it gossip, isn't it?" she snapped.

"Hey," I said. "I'm sorry if this touched a nerve. When something like this happens, everybody likes to chime in with their own personal theories about who might be involved. Ray's no different. He just never learned to control his mouth like other people do."

"And what do you think will happen if it gets back to John Donnelly that we were talking about Dallas Jenkins that way at my house? He's one of our biggest clients," she hissed.

"*You* weren't talking about Dallas Jenkins at all," I said. "You can't control what other people say about your clients, and Donnelly knows that. Besides, he's probably heard the same rumors himself a hundred times before."

"Maybe so, but the fact that they were discussing him *here* makes me feel like I somehow condoned the discussion."

"Well, it's obvious you didn't. But, Dallas Jenkins is a big boy and he made his own decisions about what to get involved in. If he really is moving drugs he doesn't deserve you being all worried about somebody sullying his reputation."

"But, we're a *law firm*. Defending people is what we do. Regardless of what everybody else is saying about them."

"Even if they're guilty of selling crack to school kids too, I guess," I said, regretting the words the millisecond they were out of my mouth.

Her eyes blazed with a wrath I hadn't seen before, but she didn't say a word.

"I'm sorry," I said. "That wasn't fair."

I tried to put my arms around her but she pulled away and wouldn't look at me.

"Listen," I said. "I've spent my whole life in law enforcement. I understand the concept of guilty until proven innocent pretty well. But, I also know that people with money and power sometimes hide behind that concept because other people are too afraid to even suspect they might have done something wrong. And I know that in most cases the truth always catches up with them. I just want you to understand that this isn't the last time you're going to hear people talking about your clients, even if they're among the rich and powerful and pay you a big retainer."

She opened her mouth and started to speak, closed it and looked off to the side, tears welling in her eyes. Wiping them away angrily, she stepped to the front door and put her hand on the doorknob.

"I can't talk about this right now," she said with a throaty whisper as she opened the door for me.

CHAPTER FOUR
pee cup

A few weeks earlier, I had been contacted about doing some work for a big multi-national conglomerate that was going to be building a power plant about an hour's drive from Elmore. My work would consist mostly of running background checks on workers and subcontractors, which was all stuff I could do without setting foot on the site where the plant was being built. But, as is often was the case when you get federal and state regulators involved in anything, the idea of keeping things simple goes right out the window. As a result, anybody doing any sort of work on the project had to pass a physical exam and be drug-tested before beginning work, and that included me. So, I was scheduled for an 8:15 a.m. appointment on Monday morning to be prodded, poked, and drained of urine.

I was familiar with the location of the Petro-Tex Medical building, a renovated and newly-stuccoed building a few blocks south of my office but had never had a reason to stop there before. A receptionist took some basic information and then gave me a clipboard with several forms of background material to fill out. The other people in the waiting room were either busy filling out similar paperwork or occupied with their cell phones.

While I waited for my name to be called, I picked up and read through one of Petro-Tex Medical's brochures that advertised services geared mostly to the local oil companies; physical exams, drug testing, breath alcohol testing, work hazard identification, occupational health evaluation and rehabilitation evaluation. The back of the brochure had a photograph of Dr. Tyler Drake, wearing a white lab coat with a stethoscope draped around his neck and looking like he stepped right out of Central Casting. I didn't recognize him as a local, but if the picture was a recent one he was probably a few years younger than me, maybe in his early forties.

Having grown up in the oil patch with a father who worked for a major oil company, and then being away from it for a few years, I had noticed a couple of changes in the oil industry when I returned to town.

One was the fact that there was an increased emphasis on safety in the oilfield which was evidenced by the fact that most oilfield companies had regular safety meetings, where employees were trained by either an in-house safety specialist or someone brought in from the outside. New businesses had sprung up, with the word *safety* included in their name, that did nothing but sell safety equipment, do safety training and help businesses navigate the complexities of Federal regulations.

The drug screening routine was the other big change I had noticed. Of course, insurance companies played a big role in establishing requirements for safety training and drug screening as a way to mitigate the risk of writing liability insurance on companies whose employees operated heavy machinery and drilled holes in the earth searching for volatile and noxious petrochemicals.

I thought these particular changes in the oil industry were interesting, because it was so different than the oilfield I had imagined while listening to stories from my dad while growing up. Back then it had seemed like danger was just part of the job and coming across somebody drunk on the job wasn't so unusual. In fact, it provided the basis for a lot of funny stories. But, I guess there were a lot of things that were pretty dangerous back then that appear routine and innocent in hindsight.

A young woman dressed in pink paisley scrubs called my name and led me down a hallway to a small room where she extracted some blood, handed me a pee cup and lid and directed me to a small bathroom. When I came out and handed her the sample container she promptly removed the lid, inserted a digital thermometer into my steaming urine and recorded something on a clipboard.

"You wouldn't believe what some people try," she said. "A few weeks ago, some woman tried to use her dog's pee."

"You're kidding," I said.

"No, I'm not. She brought it in here in a turkey baster hidden in her purse. Broke down and confessed to the whole thing when we told her we were concerned her body temperature was only sixty-eight degrees. I don't even want to think about how she got that pee from her poor dog. She didn't say, and believe me, I didn't ask."

With that, she led me to a small examination room, gave me a gown and told me the doctor would be in before long. After changing into the gown, I sat listening to the muffled sound of voices in nearby exam rooms and letting my gaze shift back and forth between a poster showing the human digestive system and another one illustrating diseases of the heart. I was briefly envious of the people I'd seen out in the lobby with their smartphones and unseen texting partners.

Finally, there was a quick double-knock on the door and Dr. Tyler Drake entered and introduced himself. The exam itself felt a bit rushed and I got the impression that the doctor may have had less concern over my health than a typical doctor would; that the primary goal of our visit was to get the paperwork done so we could both get on to more pressing matters. Being the born conversationalist that I am, I tried to engage him a few times about whether business was good or whether the Cowboys had a chance next season, but he wasn't having any of it.

"Take all the time you need getting dressed, and Maxine at the front desk can answer any questions you have about when to expect to hear something back from us."

In other words, *don't bother me with your asinine attempts at conversation, I'm a doctor for God's sake.*

Maxine at the front desk was a lot nicer and more willing to talk than Dr. Drake had been.

"Oh, business has been real

good," she said. "In fact, when they're busy in the oilfield we're twice as busy in here. Some of these guys go to work for one company and six months later get a better offer from somebody else. Well, that means they have to come right back here and get another physical and pass another drug test before they can start with the new company."

"Is that right?" I asked.

"You just wait and see," she said with a laugh. "You'll be back."

CHAPTER FIVE
no show

The week started out slowly. After leaving Petro-Tex Medical, I spent the rest of Monday and half of Tuesday morning trying to tie up loose ends on several ongoing investigations, all of them involving insurance companies, either as the hero or the villain. Tuesday afternoon I was at my desk reading through some police reports when a confused teen-aged boy opened the door between my office and Lita's dining room, walked a couple of feet inside and stopped. I glanced up and then gestured to his right.

"Next door over. You want the one that says *Caballeros* on it."

He mumbled an apology of sorts and backed out of the room. When Pete Rascon had converted one of Lita's dining rooms to office space, he provided doors leading from each of the new offices into the restaurant, apparently hoping it would encourage the tenants to dine nearby. The doors to the restrooms were on the same wall, and hardly a day went by without a restaurant patron accidentally walking into my office. I tried leaving the door locked when I was there, but when they stood there jiggling the doorknob for more than a few seconds I inevitably had to get up to open the door and give them directions. At least with it unlocked I didn't have to get up as often. And, I kept a vague hope alive in the back of my mind that an actual client might walk through the door someday.

Not thirty seconds after the teenager closed the door, it opened again. A thin young woman in her late teens or early twenties, with a toddler on her hip and a slightly older boy in tow maneuvered into the office. She glanced up at me and then closed the door behind her as she shushed the older boy and warned him to behave. I started to redirect her to the ladies' room, but she cut me off before I could.

"Excuse me, are you Buddy Griffin?"

I admitted that I was and she introduced herself as Courtney Ramey. She was dressed in a pair of faded jeans and a black T-shirt bearing the smiling face of George Strait. Her hair was somewhere between blonde and brown and hung limply to her shoulders. She didn't look any different than the typical young woman who gets pregnant early and suddenly becomes caught up in the struggle to figure out life after high school. Her brownish-green eyes had a vacant, tired look that conveyed a mixture of apathy and weariness.

After she was seated and the kids were settled, she explained that her husband, Justin Ramey was missing.

"I need somebody's help," she said. "But before we get too far into this, how much do you charge for tracking down a missing person?"

I could tell from her appearance and the way she acted that she couldn't afford to hire a private detective.

"Why don't you just tell me a little bit about the situation and then we can figure out if I can help you. How long has Justin been missing?"

"Since sometime last Tuesday."

"When did you see him last?"

"Around noon on Tuesday. I took the kids to Wal-Mart and then over to my sister's house. He was still asleep when I left, but he had to get up and go to work that afternoon. He works the evening tower, four to midnight. He was already gone by the time I got home."

"Who does he work for?"

"Jenkins Drilling. He's a roustabout."

Roustabout was a term used in the oilfield to describe the unskilled laborers working on a drilling site. Justin Ramey might spend his time on the job doing anything from painting equipment to digging ditches—typically the work that nobody else wanted to do. A hierarchy existed on every drilling rig and most of the men working in higher positions had served time as a roustabout at some point in their careers.

"You think he left for work sometime between noon and four in the afternoon on Tuesday. What was he driving?"

"He wasn't driving. He works on a drilling crew and they pick him up. Dan, that's the driller, makes the rounds every afternoon and picks up everybody in the crew at their houses, and then drops them back off after their shift ends at midnight."

She half-stood to pull the oldest boy away from a model stock car displayed on my desk.

"It works out good that way," she continued. "We've only got Justin's pickup, and I'd be left afoot with the babies if he had to take it to work."

"Does he normally come straight home from the rig?"

"Usually. Justin don't get along real well with the guys he works with, so when the rest of the crew goes out drinking or something he don't ever go with them. They've been working on a rig over by Eunice, so he usually doesn't get home until about one in the morning. I waited and waited, but he never showed up. So, I got worried, you know? I thought maybe they had a wreck or some kind of accident out at the rig."

I nodded. There were tears forming in her eyes. She blinked rapidly and collected herself as she pulled her son away from the model again and gestured for him to stay put beside her.

 "So, when it got to be daylight and he still wasn't home I called Dan's house. I was gonna ask Dan's wife if she'd heard anything. But Dan answered the phone, so I knew right away there wasn't no accident or nothing like that. I was hoping he'd tell me Justin had gone to the bar with the other guys, like maybe he finally made friends with them or something. But Dan said he hadn't seen Justin since he dropped him off at home last Monday night. He said Justin told him he'd get to the rig on his own on Tuesday. But, that don't make sense. We've only got one vehicle."

 "Have you reported Justin missing to the police?"

 "I talked to somebody on Thursday I think it was, but they

didn't seem real concerned when I first talked to them. They all know Justin down there at the police station. He's been in trouble with the law before. They acted like I should just go home and wait for him to show up, like he was just out somewhere getting into trouble. Then, a couple of detectives came by the house yesterday morning asking to talk to Justin. They didn't even know I had already reported him missing."

"Did they say what they wanted to talk to him about?"

"No, they just told me to have him contact them. They acted like I knew how to get in touch with him or something."

"Justin never said anything to you about getting to the rig any other way than riding with Dan and the rest of the crew?"

"No, and that's what don't make

sense. I know he wouldn't plan on taking his pickup because he doesn't like me being without transportation if I should need it. And, even if he did he would have made sure I was back with the pickup before he needed to leave on Tuesday afternoon. Like I said, he didn't get along with the other guys on the crew, so I know none of them would've been giving him a ride."

She looked down and began straightening out a seam on the baby's soiled T-shirt. She was searching for the right words to continue. Finally, she spoke in a low voice, choking back a sob.

"I know it sounds weird, but I don't think I believe him."

"Who?"

"Dan. His boss."

"You think he's lying about not seeing Justin on Tuesday?

"Yes," she said, looking up at me with tear-filled eyes. "I think something happened at the rig, or they did something to Justin, or there was a fight or something and they're covering it up. He never did fit in with that crew and he was always talking about arguing with Dan or somebody else. I think they're covering something up."

"Did anybody else see Dan pick him up Tuesday afternoon?"

"No. There ain't nobody else who could have seen it. But, *I know* they picked him up."

I sat back in my chair and thought for a moment. There were a number of possibilities to explain where Justin Ramey was and why he didn't come home to his family. Some of the more likely ones didn't involve violence or anything sinister at all but might be difficult for Courtney Ramey to think about.

My guess was that drugs, alcohol, money or sex played a part in Justin Ramey's disappearance. And chances were that one of those might also explain why the detectives wanted to pay him a visit.

"Let me ask you something," I said. "How long have you and Justin been married?"

"Two years. His mama made him wait 'til he finished high school. But we've been together for almost five years. He's this one's daddy," she said, pulling a stack of my business cards away from the toddler.

"And, in the time you've been together, has Justin been involved with any other women?"

She looked down at her lap and her mouth quivered slightly as she answered.

"No. Not that I know of. Justin

gets involved in a lot of things he shouldn't, but I've never caught him cheating on me. Or ever suspected that he might be."

"You mentioned that Justin has been in trouble with the law. What kind of trouble?"

"Drugs, mostly. He got busted twice for possession of pot. But, the second time it wasn't his fault. He got stopped driving a delivery truck on his last job and there was some pot wrapped in little bundles in the back. Justin didn't even know it was there. He didn't have to do no jail time though. They dropped all the charges."

"How come?"

"Oh, Justin's boss hired this bigshot lawyer and he proved that the cop who stopped him didn't have permission to search the truck. The cops are still mad over that deal. That's why they aren't that interested in looking for him."

"You said that was on his last job. Who was his boss?"

"His uncle. Benny Shanks. Justin delivered video machines for him."

What I had assumed would be a routine husband-gone-astray case got a lot more interesting at the mention of Benny Shanks' name. That Justin had disappeared so close to the time of the shooting death of his uncle was too big a coincidence to ignore, and apparently the Elmore PD felt the same way.

"I'm sure you know about what happened to Benny on Saturday night," I said. "Do you think that's why the detectives came around asking for your husband?"

"That's what I'm afraid of, that they think he had something to do with it." she said. "None of it makes sense, though. I mean

Justin got mad at Benny a few times, but they got along fine most of the time. And I know Justin couldn't have shot his own uncle. Besides, I haven't seen Justin since last Tuesday and Benny was killed Saturday night."

"How long ago did Justin work for Benny?" I asked.

"Up until about six months ago. He worked for him all through high school, first at the pawn shop and then at B & M Vending. Benny was always real good to Justin. More like a father than an uncle, I guess you might say. He was the one who suggested that Justin put in his application at Jenkins Drilling. Justin didn't think he had a chance of getting hired on, but they called him back right away. I think Benny may have pulled some strings there."

"Did Justin have any idea how the

pot ended up in the truck he was driving when he got stopped by the police?"

"He was pretty sure it was from Tyrell. That's another one of Benny's employees. Tyrell worked mostly in the bar, but sometimes Benny made him help Justin when they needed to move some of the bigger vending machines."

"Does Tyrell still work for Benny?"

"I don't know. Justin was friends with Tyrell before that incident with the pot, but I told him he needed to break it off if Tyrell was selling drugs. Especially since he was so willing to let Justin take the fall for that pot."

She paused and shook her head. "I still can't believe Benny's dead. Poor Maria, I bet she's taking it hard."

"You're close to Benny's wife?"

"Oh, yeah. I don't see her a lot,

but she was always real sweet to me whenever I came by to pick up Justin's paycheck or when we'd visit them at Christmas. She even gave me some curtains to help fix up the trailer when Justin and I first moved in together. Justin's mom wouldn't lift a finger to help us because she said we were living in sin. And, I mean, we already had a kid together and everything."

"Did you get the names of the detectives who were asking about Justin?"

"One of them gave me a card," she said, digging through her purse. "Here it is. Detective Robert Clemmer."

She passed the creased business card to me. I had become acquainted with Bob Clemmer a few months earlier when I took an interest in a murder on which he was the lead investigator. He was a good guy.

"There's no way Justin had anything to do with Benny getting killed," she said. "He may get involved in some things he shouldn't but he wouldn't hurt anybody, especially not Benny."

"Maybe the police think Justin could have seen what happened," I said. "Benny was shot in his car. Could Justin have been with him?"

"At two in the morning? There's no way. I mean, I don't want this to sound wrong or nothing, but Justin's white and he wouldn't go around that part of town at night. He just wouldn't."

"Even with Benny? It happened pretty close to A.J.'s Lounge, so maybe Benny had business there and took Justin along."

She shook her head slowly. "I don't think so. Benny would go just about anywhere at any time of the night or day, but whenever he'd take Justin with him to A.J.'s during the daytime he'd tell Justin to wait in the car and keep the doors locked and windows rolled up. And, he even warned Justin not to ever go around there by himself at night."

After going over the details of Justin's disappearance with Courtney Ramey, she asked about my rates again. I told her I would do some informal nosing around without charging anything, since it was obvious money was tight for the young couple. And, I felt like I owed it to Benny to look into the disappearance of his nephew. Benny may have lived on the wrong side of the law most of his life, but he had been an interesting character and easy to like. I figured that Justin Ramey would show up at home or contact his wife pretty soon and either way I wouldn't need to spend much time looking for him, so I made Courtney promise to keep me informed about any new developments. That's how I expected it to go anyway. Of course, things don't always go the way I expect them to..

CHAPTER SIX
big boss man

Dan Cunningham, the driller on whose crew Justin Ramey worked, lived in an older brick home four blocks west of Main Street in an area that had been in a gradual decline for decades. The lack of any zoning laws in Elmore had resulted in a patchwork of residences mixed with commercial buildings in some of the blocks close to downtown. Dan Cunningham's home was large and well-maintained, but the curb-appeal went straight to hell when you glanced over at the long-abandoned car wash next door.

I wasn't sure what time would be best to drop by and talk to Cunningham with the odd hours that he worked, but luckily, he was standing in his front yard when I drove up. He was dressed in work pants and a white undershirt, smoking a cigarette while he used a garden hose to spray water back and forth on his sun-scorched front lawn. A white crew-cab pickup with the Jenkins Drilling logo on the door sat in the driveway. I parked my own pickup at the curb.

"We don't get some rain soon I think we're all gonna dry up and blow away," I said, extending my hand. "Buddy Griffin."

"Aw, shit," he said, looking down at the water hose in his hand as if he'd just realized he was holding it.

"I'm just out here to smoke. My wife's emphysema acts up if I smoke inside. Dan Cunningham."

I gave him one of my business cards and told him I was trying to help find Justin Ramey. He studied the front of the card with a smirk on his face, glancing at the back of it before looking up.

"Justin Ramey," he repeated flatly, as if he'd never heard the name before. "I don't know nothing about him."

He turned his back and started pulling the water hose toward the house signaling our conversation was finished.

"Well, I know he works for Jenkins Drilling and I know you're his supervisor. I was hoping you might be able to give me some details about the last time you saw him."

He stopped and turned around to

face me.

"He may have worked for Jenkins Drilling in the past, but he don't anymore. If you need any more information I suggest you talk to Sheryl in Human Resources."

"What do you mean?"

He shrugged and tossed the hose away from him and started walking toward the faucet where the hose was connected.

"He was fired." I could see he was weighing whether to say more.

"Some of these kids think they can handle working out in the field and turns out they can't," he said. "When they don't show up for work and don't call anybody to let them know, we've got to replace them. I've already filled Justin's spot."

"What time did you pick Justin up at his house on Tuesday afternoon?"

He gave me a tired look, as if I'd

already asked the same question ten times before.

"Listen, I already talked to Justin's wife about this. I really don't have time to go over it all again."

"How was Justin on the job site? Did he get along okay with the rest of the crew?"

He bent to turn off the faucet and then stood looking at me for a few seconds. He took a long drag on what was left of his cigarette and flipped it towards the street.

"Listen, every new guy I've ever put on had to take some crap from the other guys. That's just part of it. I don't allow things to get out of hand though, or everybody involved gets shit-canned."

"Was he a good worker?"

"He wasn't bad, but he hadn't been around a rig much before, so he didn't know what was going on most of the time. A drilling rig is a dangerous place and I don't have a lot of time to spend babysitting the new hands. To tell you the truth I'd rather have a lazy son of a bitch who knows what's going on out there than somebody like Justin that might do something to get himself killed."

"Did Justin tell you how he intended to get to the drilling location on Tuesday afternoon?"

He looked off toward the street for a second and then turned and began walking away.

"Was somebody else planning on giving him a ride that day?" I said.

Instead of responding, Cunningham went inside the house and closed the front door, leaving me alone on the front lawn. While it was obvious he wasn't too concerned over the whereabouts of Justin Ramey he did seem to be going out of his way to keep from telling me everything he knew about the disappearance. And, his reluctance just made me that much more interested in finding out what had really happened.

CHAPTER SEVEN
granny mo

As I drove away from Dan Cunningham's house, I decided to take a look at where Justin and Courtney Ramey lived, since I really didn't have much else to do that might help me locate Justin. I figured I'd pay a visit to Jenkins Drilling eventually, but I didn't want to go there too early. For one thing, I wanted to give Justin a little more time to show up at home. And, the extra time could work to my advantage if there was something going on that somebody was trying to hide. It would give those involved time to worry about what they'd done, and that kind of worry sometimes caused panic and mistakes. And mistakes sometimes provide an investigator with their best leads.

The Rameys lived on the south end of town close to the city limits in an area dominated by commercial oilfield activity. There were one or two active oilfield-related companies nearby, but more than half of the buildings in the surrounding blocks appeared to be empty or only used as warehouses. Justin and Courtney Ramey lived in an older mobile home, one of three parked next to a grassy lot filled with rusting oilfield equipment and surrounded by a chain link fence topped with barbed wire.

I parked on the street around the corner from the Ramey home and climbed the steps on the rusted steel platform that served as a front porch to their trailer. I knocked several times, even though I wasn't optimistic about finding anybody home, since the rutted dirt driveway leading from the street to the trailer space was empty. As I was standing there at the door waiting, I looked around at the surrounding trailers and buildings. It was quiet, but I knew there were probably eyes watching me from somewhere nearby. I was dressed in a white western shirt, brown slacks, boots and wearing a straw Stetson, which gave the impression that I might be a deputy sheriff or somebody in law enforcement. It was an impression that sometimes helped avoid confrontation when I visited neighborhoods like the one where Justin and Courtney Ramey lived. But, it was also an impression that made people clam up and vanish indoors whenever I rolled up on a location. I hadn't really planned on trying to dig too deeply into Justin Ramey's disappearance today, but if I did decide to talk to the neighbors I would probably dress down a little bit and maybe play the part of an oilfield boss looking to offer Justin a spot on a work crew. People were more willing to talk if they thought they might be helping their neighbor out instead of ratting them out to the cops.

As I started down the steps of the steel porch I glanced up and noticed an elderly woman sitting in an old-fashioned wooden swing that hung from the rafters of a front porch halfway down the block and across the street from the

Ramey trailer. I watched her as I walked to my pickup and could tell she was watching me right back. So, I altered my course and began walking towards her. I waved as I stepped onto her lawn and she raised a hand in answer.

"How you doing?" I shouted. "It's been another hot day."

"You're right about that," she answered, smiling. "I try to stay up here out of the sun as much as I can this time of year."

The house was a small neatly-kept wooden-sided dwelling that looked like it might have been an oilfield camp house originally, built on company land decades earlier to house workers and then later sold by the company and moved into town. Such houses were common in Elmore and the surrounding oilfield towns in the region where housing had been scarce before the oil boom hit and the oil companies needed to construct cheap shelter for their men close to the wells they drilled.

"I was hoping to catch Mrs. Ramey at home but I guess she's not there," I said.

"No, I saw her leaving about an hour ago with both of them kids of theirs. That boy Caleb comes over here to see me sometimes."

"What about Mr. Ramey? Have you seen him around?"

She looked off towards the Ramey trailer while she thought about her answer.

"Not in a few days," she said, finally. "Not that it's any of my business, but I was wondering if he's gotten himself in some trouble."

"Really? Why's that, ma'am?"

"Seen a couple of plainclothes cops over there a time or two, talking to Courtney. Thought that might be why Justin hasn't been around lately."

"How did you know they were cops?" I asked.

She laughed softly and gave a lazy swat at a fly that was taking turns buzzing the two of us.

"Oh, I can recognize most of the cops around here. I'm out here on this porch most of the time when I ain't asleep and they all drive by here eventually. I learn to recognize their faces and watch 'em climb up the ranks, from the patrol cars to the plain little unmarked cars to the bigger and fancier unmarked cars. Course, by the time they're driving those big fancy ones, they don't come around nearly as much. But now you, I can tell you ain't no cop."

"Oh, really? How's that?" Maybe my deputy sheriff disguise wasn't working as well as I thought it was.

"Well, I never seen you before, and you're old enough I would've seen you plenty of times if you would've come up through the ranks."

"Well, you're right," I said. "I'm not a cop."

I reached in my shirt pocket and handed her a business card.

"My name's Buddy Griffin, ma'am. I'm a private detective."

She took it and studied it.

"Pleased to meet you," she answered. "Maureen Wright, but nobody's called me Maureen in years. Mostly I go by Granny Mo, cause that's what my grandbabies used to call me, before they all grew up. Now their babies call me that."

"It's a pleasure to meet you Granny Mo. So, you see pretty much everything that goes on around here, huh?"

"I see it all Mr. Griffin, the good, the bad, and the ugly. Is that Justin in some kind of trouble with the law?"

"I sure hope not, ma'am. But he hasn't been home since last Tuesday and Courtney's worried that something might have happened to him."

"Last Tuesday? Oh, my. That doesn't sound good, does it?"

"No ma'am it doesn't. I know it's been a week, but do you remember seeing any cars or pickups over at the Rameys' on that day?"

"Oh Lord, I'm lucky if I can tell you what day it is today and what I had for supper last night. I'm sorry Mr. Griffin, but I'm not going to be much help to you."

"Have you ever noticed a pickup stopping at the house to pick Justin up?"

"Sure, I have. A white one, the kind that has a back seat and an extra door. I'm pretty sure it's a Jenkins Drilling truck. Usually picks him up in the afternoon if I'm not mistaken."

"But, you can't say for sure you saw it last Tuesday?"

"No, I'm sorry I can't. It could have stopped to pick him up that day, or it could have been that other vehicle that picks him up sometimes."

"You mean something besides the white Jenkins Drilling crew cab?"

"Yes sir. There's a big SUV stops there on some days about the same time and Justin comes out and gets in it, dressed in the same coveralls he wears when he gets in the white pickup."

"An SUV? Do you remember what color it was?"

"Seems like it might have been red. Or maybe brown. I'm really not sure to tell you the truth. But, I do remember it had one of those personalized license plates on it."

"Do you remember what was on the license plate?"

"No, I don't. I'm sorry"

"But this red or brown SUV stopped for Justin more than once?" I asked.

"I'd say there's been at least a dozen times I saw it stop there," she answered. "Not real regular, but often enough to notice. Maybe once a week or something like that."

CHAPTER EIGHT
pawn shop

After thanking Granny Mo for the information, I drove around aimlessly for a while thinking about Justin Ramey and the fact that he disappeared so close to the time of the murder of his uncle. But, what did that mean? Could Justin have been responsible for Benny's shooting? Something told me that the more I learned about Benny Shanks and the events leading up to his murder, the better chance I had of finding a link to Justin

Ramey in there somewhere.

I had seen Benny Shanks' obituary in the Elmore Sentinel earlier that morning and learned that Benny had already been buried in a Jewish cemetery in Odessa, about 25 miles south of Elmore. I wasn't completely clear on Jewish customs but knew that it might not be proper for me to pay a visit to Benny's widow, Maria Schankowitz, at their home during the mourning period, so I drove by the pawn shop to see if it was open for business.

Benny's Pawn and Loan was located in a large cinderblock building that it shared with another of Benny Shanks' enterprises, B & M Vending. A newer, stucco-covered building sat next door and housed the newest addition to Benny's businesses; Field Hands Employment Agency, which specialized in placing oilfield workers in temporary and permanent positions.

Benny's Pawn and Loan had been in the same location for several decades and I had visited the place dozens of times during my high school years to dig through the treasure-trove of old used record albums, cassettes and 8-track tapes that Benny had for sale. Benny's records and tapes could also be traded for on a two-for-one basis, and during my teenage years I didn't have much cash to spare but could always come up with two not-so-good albums or tapes that I'd gladly trade for one really good one. My parents frowned on my going to Benny's pawn shop, since Benny was almost always under investigation for accepting stolen merchandise, but they knew my love of music was the only reason for my visits.

The inside of Benny's Pawn and Loan was a little different from my last visit almost thirty years earlier, but not much. The shelves of albums and tapes that had dominated one entire wall of the shop were gone and the display cases had been rearranged, but some things about the place remained the same. The same musty smell hung in the air, with undertones of stale cigarette smoke and oilfield grease, probably from tools that had disappeared from a drilling location somewhere nearby and been hocked for enough cash to finance a weekend drinking binge.

Nobody was behind the counter and I was the only customer, so I browsed the aisles for a few minutes until I heard a woman's voice behind me.

"All the stuff on that side of the room is twenty percent off what it's marked," she said.

I turned and immediately recognized Maria Schankowitz, although I was looking at a slightly heavier and weathered version of the attractive woman I had dealt with on a regular basis back in my music trading days. Back then, I thought she was pretty hot in an exotic sort of way, with her jet-black beehive hairdo, lots of eye makeup and the rumors that she'd been a stripper in Dallas before marrying Benny. She'd always had an aura of toughness to her, which had been reinforced by the fact that she kept Benny's small empire running smoothly when he was away doing a couple of stretches in the state pen for income tax evasion and food-stamp fraud.

"Mrs. Schankowitz?" I asked,

stepping up to the glass display case she stood behind and offering my hand. "I'm Buddy Griffin. I'm so sorry for your loss."

"Why, thank you," she said. Her hand was soft and cool when we shook.

"You probably don't remember me, but I used to be a regular customer here about a hundred years ago."

"I do remember you," she said. "Benny mentioned that you'd moved back to town. He was still mad at you for winning all those games back when you played for the Drillers."

I laughed. "Now, I told him when I talked to him out at The Pumpjack Club that he should have never been betting against us back in those days."

"Well, he didn't have a lot of choice," she said. "Everybody in town wanted to put some money on you boys and he had to either cover the action or get out of the business."

"I'm only sorry I never got a chance to make it up to him," I said. "Is there anything I can do for you?"

"No, I'm doing okay," she said. "I know it doesn't look right for me to be down here working this soon, but I go crazy when I don't have something to do. I don't know if you knew it, but Benny was Jewish and we buried him right away which is their custom, but that's as far as I go with that stuff. I was raised a Catholic and I always made sure we had a Christmas tree right along with the menorah every year."

The door from the street opened and a black man in his late twenties wearing an expensive looking Los Angeles Lakers throwback jersey entered and walked around behind the counter. He was carrying a worn bank deposit bag with Elmore National Bank printed on it. He nodded at me and glanced around the shop.

"Everything okay?" he asked Maria.

"Yeah," she said. "Did you go by the club?"

"Yes ma'am. Janet said she'd stay there even if Chrissy didn't show up tonight."

"Okay, good," she answered. And then to me: "You wouldn't believe what a pain in the ass it is trying to find a reliable bartender."

"I hear you," I said. "I put myself through college tending bar down in Austin, and it was hard back then even with a town full of college kids to draw from."

"You didn't get a football

scholarship?" she asked.

"I did but got hurt and couldn't play. My folks couldn't pick up the tab at a school like UT, so I had to come up with some other way to pay for it."

"You got any kids of your own?" she asked.

"A daughter in medical school in Lubbock," I said.

"That's gotta be expensive."

"Oh, it is, but her mother's folks had their heart set on sending their granddaughter to their alma mater and insisted on helping out."

"Sounds like you married well."

"Yep," I said, laughing. "And divorced well too."

"Been there, done that. Benny and I never had any children. But, I never wanted any, and Benny didn't seem to miss having kids."

"I met a young woman named Courtney Ramey the other day," I

said. "She mentioned that her husband was Benny's nephew. Justin?"

"That's right. Courtney's a sweet girl, and Benny treated Justin like he was his own son."

"When I talked to her, she was worried about Justin. He hasn't been home in a few days and she hasn't heard anything from him."

"Is that right?" she said. "I tell you, those two have gone at it like cats and dogs ever since they started going out together, so it doesn't surprise me if he walked out on her. I'm sure he'll turn up in a day or two and they'll patch things up."

"I hope so," I said. "But, she seems to think there's more to it than that. She doesn't think he disappeared on his own, that something might have happened on his job. She also said that

Benny was the one who suggested Justin apply for work at Jenkins Drilling. Did Benny help him get his job there?"

"If he did I never knew anything about it," she said. "But, there was a lot about what Benny did that I never knew about. Not that he was keeping things from me, but it's just how he did things. What I didn't know couldn't hurt me sort of a thing. I'm sure you've heard plenty of rumors about Benny, being an ex-cop and all."

"I've heard a few," I said. "I guess it must make it kind of hard to carry on with the business if you didn't know what Benny was doing."

"Oh, I know enough about the pawn shop and the vending business to keep them running, and I've got good people running the Pumpjack Club and Field

Hands. But, those are the only parts of Benny's business that I know about. He kept a lot of things from me to protect me, you know. I just hope I can make enough money to make ends meet without the extra cash all that sneaky stuff used to bring in. That's what I always called it when Benny and I talked about it, *sneaky stuff*. I always said that sneaky stuff was gonna get him in trouble again, I just figured it would mean some more time in jail, and not getting his damn head blown off."

She said that last part matter-of-factly and emotionless, as if Benny had simply missed the point spread on a big game and come out losing money instead of his life.

"What do you think happened?" I asked.

"I don't know and don't really

care. When we were younger, I always figured it would be that part of Benny's life that would kill him sooner or later, but why'd it have to wait until he was an old man? Half the people his age are already gone from heart attacks or cancer or something. But, when you're doing what he was doing there's always competition, somebody who wants to take away your customers."

"Who was Benny's competition?" I asked. "Somebody local?"

She shrugged. "Could be. He might have gotten crossways with somebody in A.J.'s posse. That would be my guess, considering where he was when he got shot."

A.J. Lipscomb was the owner of A.J.'s Lounge, where the police shootout had taken place that stirred up such a political controversy. I had heard rumors that A.J. was involved in some of the same illegal activities that Benny Shanks had built his career on.

"To tell you the truth," she continued. "His girlfriend would know more about that part of his business than I would."

"A.J.'s girlfriend?" I asked.

"No. Benny's girlfriend. Her name's Madison Miller and she and Benny started seeing each other years ago. Benny didn't think I knew about her, but you can't keep nothing secret in this town for very long."

"So, you were okay with it?"

"Hell no, but I decided that if I made him give her up he'd just find another one to replace her. Once a cheater, always a cheater is how I looked at it. At least this way, I knew her name and could keep tabs on him easier."

"Does she live here in Elmore?"

"Yeah, she does. She sells cars down at the Chevrolet house when she's not out screwing married men. Hey, do me a favor, will you? If you talk to her, tell her you think Benny had another girlfriend over on Avenue B he was going to visit that night."

She laughed. "That'll give her a little something to think about."

CHAPTER NINE
oh, by the way

Norris Jackson's police cruiser with the word *SHERIFF* emblazoned on the side in foot-high letters was parked in front of *Lita's Little Mexico Restaurant* when I got back to the office. When I unlocked the street entrance door to my office, I found Norris waiting inside. He was sitting at my desk with a magazine open in front of him, along with a basket of tortilla chips, a bowl of salsa and a glass of iced tea he'd carried over from Lita's next door.

"Has there been a break-in?" I asked, helping myself to the basket of chips. I noticed that Norris had dug until he found the *Sports Illustrated Swimsuit Issue* in the stack of several dozen sports and gun magazines I kept in a corner behind the desk.

"It amazes me how these people can take the same subject and cover it pretty much the same way year after year and still manage to make it seem fresh and interesting," he said.

"You know, you can take that with you if you're in the middle of a story or something," I told him.

"That's okay," he said, closing the magazine. "Probably get me in trouble at home."

"Dolores doesn't appreciate fine sports coverage?"

"She's just real narrow-minded

when it comes to what sporting events she thinks are worth following. Listen Buddy, I've needed to tell you something, and I don't know any other way but to flat out tell you. But, I hope you'll respect my wishes to keep this confidential."

I sat down in the guest chair in front of the desk.

"Sure, Norris. I can keep a secret. You know that," I said.

Norris was leaning forward, his folded arms on the desk and a look on his face that made me think he might be about to reveal the location of Jimmy Hoffa's body.

"I owed Benny Shanks some money," he said. "A whole lot of money. More money than I have any business owing anybody unless I borrowed it to buy a house or something."

"And I'm guessing you didn't use

it to buy a house," I said.

"No sir, I didn't," he continued. "Bet it all on basketball, football and hell, even baseball. Can you imagine that? A fully-grown and supposedly intelligent man betting money on a damn baseball game?"

"How much are we talking about?"

He looked down at the desk, unable to meet my eyes. This was difficult for him.

"Twenty-seven thousand, give or take. And, of course the meter runs on it every damn minute that it ain't paid back."

"So, that's why you wanted me to look into the shooting instead of looking into it yourself."

He nodded.

"If this gets out I'm screwed, aren't I?" he said.

"I don't know," I said. "Depends on how it comes out, and if anybody wants to try to make something out of it."

"So, what should I do? Resign?"

"That's something you've got to decide for yourself," I said. "Have you found out who's working the murder and talked to them about it?"

"No. You're the first person I've talked to. I haven't even told Dolores yet."

"Don't you think you'd better?"

"I know, I know. This is just so damn embarrassing. I thought I had a handle on things, I really did. I've even gone to some Gambler's Anonymous meetings in Midland."

"Who's the lead detective on the case?" I asked.

"I'm pretty sure it's Bob Clemmer."

"Well, at least it's somebody who knows you," I said. "That's one good thing."

"Jesus, you think those guys will be looking at me for the shooting?"

I hated to answer the question, but not answering it honestly wouldn't have been doing Norris any favors.

"If it was my investigation, and I found out you owned Benny a pile of money, I'd certainly have to take a look at you, Norris. Of course, if you came to me first and told me about the debt it would go a long way to reducing the suspicion level. No cop alive is so squeaky clean that they can't understand another cop getting into trouble with gambling or drinking. And, I think Clemmer's a pretty realistic guy when it comes to understanding human behavior."

"You're right, I've got to talk to him, don't I?"

"And, the sooner the better, I'd

say."

He stared at the top of the desk for a few seconds before pushing back and standing up.

"I appreciate your honesty Buddy, I really do. I guess I've got to face up to what I've done and take whatever comes as a result. But, I'd still appreciate it if you'd keep it under your hat until I've told Dolores and had a chance to sit down with Clemmer."

"Of course," I said standing and shaking hands. "Norris, I hope you understand that if I do happen to find out something about the shooting, I may not be sharing all of it with you. You need to stay as far away from any investigation into Benny Shanks' murder as you can right now."

CHAPTER TEN
proposal

The lead story on the front page of Thursday morning's Elmore Sentinel was Benny Shanks' murder, and political candidate Cleve Campbell was already busy trying to use the shooting to add steam to his crusade against the Elmore Police Department. Campbell had stood up and made a speech at a meeting of the Elmore City Commission, calling again for another independent investigation into the shooting at A.J.'s Lounge that had taken place eight months before. He cited Benny Shanks' murder as evidence that police don't offer any protection to the citizens in the black neighborhoods of Elmore. The article mentioned that Police Chief Adams was not available for comment following the meeting.

After I finished reading the morning papers, I called Courtney Ramey to see if she knew anything more about her husband's disappearance, and to make sure he hadn't miraculously reappeared without her telling me about it. She didn't have any news for me so I decided to pay a visit to the Elmore Police Department and talk to Detective Bob Clemmer. I knew Norris probably hadn't had time to meet with him and discuss his personal connection to Benny Shanks' bookmaking business, but if I was going to be asking questions around town about Benny's nephew Justin Ramey and about Benny's own activities, I thought it was wise to let Clemmer know about it up front.

The Elmore PD was located in a two-story stucco-covered building on the edge of the town square. I had vivid memories of going into the building when it had been a G.F. Wacker five and dime store with wooden floors and slowly turning ceiling fans hanging from long rods. When I was a kid, I probably spent a good portion of any allowance I was ever given on toys or candy from that store. After it sat empty for a few years, the City of Elmore bought the building and had it renovated for use as police headquarters. Now the exterior was all modern angles and mirrored windows. The reflective coating on the windows was probably there to filter the heat from the brutal west Texas sun, but it made me think of a two-way mirror in an interrogation room.

Inside the building there wasn't a trace remaining of anything that might conjure up a memory of Wacker's toy department or lunch counter. Instead, visitors found themselves in a sterile, brightly-lit entry room separated from the workings of the department by bullet-proof glass. It was a distinctly different experience than walking in the front door of the Sheriff's office to visit Norris. There, I was able to wander in past the receptionist and make my way back to Norris' office on my own. Here, I had to tell the receptionist behind the glass exactly who I was and exactly who I needed to see.

After a few minutes, Bob Clemmer came through the door that led into the inner sanctum carrying a leather satchel. He let the door close behind him.

"Buddy Griffin, you must have read my mind. I've been thinking about calling you," Clemmer said as we shook hands.

"Well, I hope I don't need my attorney present," I said.

"No, no. Nothing like that. You have time for a cup of coffee?"

"Sure," I said, starting toward where I knew the employee break room was.

"What, you were going to drink the coffee here?" he said. "Are you kidding? We only serve that to suspects to break them down during interrogation. Let's go across the street."

With that we left the modern, antiseptic environment of Elmore

Police Headquarters behind and walked down the street to Bagel Barn, which was a tiny sandwich shop on the town square. Inside were a few small tables and the smell of freshly-baked cookies in the air.

"I'm sure you already know, but Benny Shanks' nephew went missing a few days before Benny was shot," I said after we were sitting down with coffee and Texas-sized white chocolate chip macadamia nut cookies.

"Justin Ramey?" he said. "We looked at him to see if he might have been mixed up in it somehow, but nothing really jumped out at us. Seems like he's basically a good kid who's gotten in a little trouble, but what kid hasn't?"

"His wife came to see me," I said. She wanted me to try to help find him."

"Yeah, we were going to question him but she said he hadn't been home in a few days. My guess is some shapely young thing made him forgot all about his wife and kids. You remember what it was like when you were his age," Clemmer said.

"That was my thought," I said. "So, I haven't been digging too deep yet. But, I wanted to give you a heads-up in case something leads back to Benny Shanks. And, I may also be asking around about Benny too, in case there's some kind of connection."

"I appreciate you telling me," Clemmer said. "I can sure use any information you come across that relates. The Chief would like Benny's murder wrapped up pronto since it took place so close to A.J.'s."

"I understand. I saw the paper

this morning," I said.

Clemmer shook his head and chuckled under his breath.

"Cleve Campbell," he said. "Can you believe this guy, making our department his pet project? And, my money says he wouldn't even give a rip if he weren't running for office."

"Is there anything there?" I asked.

Clemmer shrugged. "Could the officers on the scene have handled the situation at A.J.'s better? Sure. But, hindsight's twenty-twenty and in the heat of the moment reactions take over. Remember, our guys weren't the only ones doing the shooting that night."

"What does Campbell really want? Didn't the DPS already do a pretty thorough investigation?"

"Of course, they did. Campbell just wants headlines and a

reputation as a crusader standing up for the little people. He needed a cause and he picked us."

"And, now you've got Benny's shooting in the same neighborhood to work. Are you getting any cooperation from witnesses?"

"Nada. The weather was nice that night, and there are always people out on the street in that block at that hour but nobody saw the shooting or heard anything."

"So, no suspects at this point?"

He didn't answer but smiled as he looked at me.

"You miss it, don't you? Working murders."

I shrugged. "I guess so. Hard not to miss something you spent most of your adult life doing."

"I can understand," he said. "People who've never worked a murder case don't understand what it's like. How that need to know what happened can take over and won't let you rest until you've followed up on every lead and explored every possibility."

"It's as bad as any obsession I've ever seen," I admitted.

"And, that's part of the reason I wanted to talk to you. Why I was glad to see you show up at the station," he said. "I've got an idea I wanted to run by you."

"What's it about?" I asked.

"I don't know whether you know it or not, but we've had some pretty deep budget cuts over the past couple of years. I'm sure you remember I used to have a partner to work cases with."

"Reese Puckett? How could I forget?" I said. "He threatened to kick my ass on more than one occasion. What happened to him?"

"He took a job in East Texas. He really wasn't a people person, was he?　Anyway, when Puckett left they decided they couldn't afford to replace him, so I'm working mostly on my own these days.　Then this shooting at A.J.'s heats things up to the point where people just don't want to cooperate with any kind of investigation if it means talking to the Elmore Police Department.　It seems like I'm spending a lot of time spinning my wheels and not getting any traction.　And Chief Adams is taking a lot of crap about the shooting, so my problems are not at the top of his list of priorities. I tried to have a sit-down with him earlier in the week and his advice to me was to think outside the box. So, I'm doing just that."

"With this idea you mentioned."

He nodded.

"Okay, bear with me here," he said.　"Put yourself in my position, working a murder case alone, or maybe with a little help from somebody without any homicide experience. You don't have anybody to bounce theories off of, or to talk to about things as they develop. You don't have anybody to pursue one lead while you're looking into another one. The clock is ticking just like it always does on a murder, but you're moving half as fast as you usually do because you're only one person."

"Sounds like a way to accumulate a lot of open cases," I said.

"Exactly. And, add to that the problem of the public holding out on us because of this fiasco at A.J.'s and it just gets worse."

He sat up straight and quickly glanced around the room, lowering his voice.

"But, if you're in this situation I've

described and you have a chance to work with somebody with lots of experience who wouldn't be perceived as part of the Elmore Police Department out on the street, don't you think it could make a tremendous difference in whether you solve the thing or not?"

"Sure, it would," I said.

"So," he said, leaning back and smiling. "What do you think?"

"About what?"

"About sticking your toe back in the water on the Benny Shanks investigation," he said. "Now I'm not talking about putting you directly on the payroll, since the budget won't allow for that. But, there's not any reason I couldn't pay you under the table for doing a little freelance investigation work. We pay snitches all the time for information, so why not pay somebody who could really give us something we could use?"

I had to admit the idea had a certain appeal to it. I really did miss working murder cases and having the Elmore PD as another source of work wouldn't hurt my fledgling PI firm's cash flow.

"So, what happens if I come across something that helps in the case? You cite me as a confidential informant in your reports?"

"Something like that. Depends on what you find and how you find it, I guess. With Benny Shanks being Justin Ramey's uncle, the fact that you're already looking for Justin and asking questions about him and his activities is perfect. If it comes down to it, instead of citing you as a CI, you could always testify directly that you came across evidence relating to Benny Shanks' murder while investigating

Justin Ramey's disappearance. There's nothing dishonest about that."

After a little more discussion, we agreed that I would give Clemmer's idea a try on the Benny Shanks murder and then evaluate whether it could be expanded to other cases later on. We spent another half hour hashing out the details of how our new relationship would work and then he reached down and picked up his satchel.

"Sorry about the cloak and dagger stuff," he said. "But I think it's better if we meet somewhere else besides headquarters."

He reached inside the satchel and pulled out a thick manila envelope.

"I can't let you have my actual case file, so these are your copies," he said, sliding it across the table. "Of course, you can't show this to anybody or let anybody know you have it."

"Understood," I said, looking down at the envelope. "How did you know I would agree to this?"

"Just a hunch," he said.

We walked back down the street to the Elmore PD Headquarters. As we stood outside the building, our conversation came back around to the details Benny Shanks' murder.

"Does your gut tell you anything about who might have shot Benny?" I asked.

"Not really. And, you know with Benny's long-standing reputation for being a smartass son-of-a-bitch, it could be that he just happened to piss-off the wrong person about something minor and they pulled their gun rather than stand there and take it. Could be somebody that's never even been on our radar screens."

"Any advice on where to start?" I

asked.

"Well, there's not a whole lot in the file yet, but you've been doing this long enough to know to look at the businesses. The pawn shop, Pumpjack Club and Field Hands. Oh, and I heard a rumor that he might have something to do with that medical clinic that does all that drug testing that all the oil companies require now."

"Petro-Tex?"

"Yeah, that's it."

"Okay. Well, I'll keep you posted if I come up with anything," I said.

"Appreciate it, Buddy. I need all the help I can get on this one."

CHAPTER ELEVEN
maybe, just maybe

Not quite an hour later I was sitting at my desk with the contents of Clemmer's file on the Benny Shanks investigation spread out in front of me. I had read through the reports and was starting to review the photos taken at the crime scene, which Clemmer had burned onto a thumb drive for me. I had just opened the drive on my computer and brought up the first picture when I suddenly remembered the Texas Brain

Freeze cup that Cuatro had given me four days earlier. What made me remember the cup was something I saw in that first photo. It was taken from about twenty feet away, facing the drivers' door of Benny Shanks' 1968 Cadillac Eldorado, which was parked along the curb, with Benny slumped in the drivers' seat. A few feet out in the street from the car was a dark puddle of something. There were two long, fingers coming from the puddle where some of the liquid had run downhill from the crest of the street toward the curb and disappeared underneath the Eldorado.

I looked closer. Was I imagining that bluish tinge to the dark stain in the photo? I quickly clicked through the remaining pictures but there weren't any that gave a better view of the stain or helped determine its true color. I walked over to the filing cabinet and looked at the Brain Freeze cup again. Could there be some connection between the cup and Benny Shanks' murder? It seemed like an impossible stroke of luck or an extremely unlikely coincidence that there would be a relationship. But, I'd seen stranger coincidences affect cases I worked in the past, so I wasn't ruling anything out.

I sat back down and began again with the first photo and went through all of the remaining ones trying to pick out any details that possibly might turn out to be important. It was a slow and methodical process, with a lot of going back and forth between photos to try to puzzle out any clues as to what happened to Benny that night. One curious thing was that the passenger door wasn't quite completely closed. There wasn't anything in the file to indicate it had been opened after the shooting by a witness or responding officer, so that left open the possibility that someone had been in the passenger seat and had left without closing the door completely.

I checked the coroner's report again. The bullet that killed Benny had entered his skull just behind his left ear and exited near his right eye socket.

"Boom, boom, boom, boom!" Cuatro had said just before he had given me the empty cup. Of course, Cuatro would have described a single 'boom' the same way.

Blood and tissue from the exit wound had sprayed the inside of the windshield on the right passenger side, where the bullet struck and shattered the glass before ending up inside the vehicle. The trajectory probably meant that Benny had his head turned slightly toward the passenger when he was shot from someone outside the vehicle.

I looked at the photo with the dark puddle again and stood up to look at the Brain Freeze cup. There was only one sure fire way to determine if the cup was connected to the stain in the photo, and that would be to turn it over to Bob Clemmer and have it looked at by the state crime lab. But, before I did that, I thought it was time for me to take a look at the site of Benny's murder.

Avenue B was less than a mile from the courthouse square, but the surrounding neighborhood was considerably different. The houses that lined the street were older and the majority not maintained very well. An old car with the windows broken out sat beside the house directly across the street from where Benny's Cadillac had been parked the night of his murder. A pit bull with cropped ears chained to a porch two houses down barked and yelped as he ran back and forth, kicking up the loose red dirt of the bare front yard and straining at the length of his chain. The house that Benny had parked directly in front of had boarded up windows and a weathered condemned property notice tacked to the front door.

I knew from studying the crime scene photos exactly where Benny's car had been parked. It hadn't rained in Elmore in months, so it wasn't hard to locate the dark stain I had seen the image of. I took several photos with my cell phone and then used a swab to gather some of the residue. Whatever left the stain was blue alright, and it was the same shade as the dried droplets inside the Texas Brain Freeze cup back at my office.

I called Clemmer and told him about the cup and the possible relation to the stain at the crime scene. He told me he'd meet me the next day to pick up the cup and have someone take samples from the stain.

CHAPTER TWELVE
barber shop

After I left the scene of Benny's murder, I decided to stop at Virgil's Barber Shop for a haircut. The shop was run by Virgil Slater III and had been opened in the 1920's by his grandfather, the original Virgil that named the shop. Virgil's was a true anachronism, existing in an age when hair stylists typically handle both men and women and often with televisions and loud music to add to the experience. I'd received most of my haircuts at

Virgil's when I was growing up, and the place hadn't changed much since my first visit more than thirty years earlier. There was still a long line of chrome and green leatherette chairs along one wall of the rectangular room, facing three evenly spaced barber chairs that were several decades older than I was. Only one of the chairs got steady use nowadays, but Virgil's was still a place where you could take the pulse of what was going on in Elmore. A stack of magazines was there for those rare times when a customer had to wait for a haircut, but they were mostly read by visitors who came by to sit and shoot the bull as part of their daily routine.

When I walked in Virgil was sitting in his barber chair with a cup of coffee in one hand and a copy of the Elmore Sentinel in the other.

"A live one!" Virgil shouted, slapping his thigh with the folded newspaper. "I was wondering how I was going to pay the light bill this month."

"How's it going, Virgil?"

"Ah, not too bad. I'm doing better than Benny Shanks, rest in peace."

"Yeah, that was quite a surprise, to me at least," I said. "Of course, I wasn't following all of Benny's activities over the years after I moved away. I still think about him as a guy making money reselling stolen car stereos."

"Oh, no. Benny branched out into all sorts of stuff after you left," he said, as we changed places and he fastened an apron around my neck.

"I would have thought he might have retired from all that by now," I said.

"Guys in Benny's line of work

don't always get to choose when they retire," he said. "Somebody else chooses for them. Talk around town is that he was in business with a big money backer. Could be that Benny wasn't able to give them the return on their investment that he promised."

"Any idea who his backer might have been?" I asked.

I wasn't sure he had heard my question, but after weighing his answer for a few seconds, he spoke in a hushed voice even though we were the only ones in the shop.

"People around here have been saying for a long time that Dallas Jenkins was mixed up in some kind of drug running operation. I know for a fact that he and a bunch of his buddies used to get together and sniff cocaine back when he was younger."

"There was a lot of that going around a few years ago," I said.

I watched him working on my hair in the deep green pool created by the endless cascade of reflections in the mirrors that faced each other and ran the entire length of the barber shop. When I was a boy I always thought that maybe if you looked deep enough into that green tunnel if you might just be able to see all of the other boys and men who had sat in that same chair getting their hair cut in the past.

"Course I'm only repeating the amateur detectives that come in here with it all figured out," he said. "Personally, I think it was probably more likely somebody with a lot less to lose than Dallas Jenkins. Benny was involved in a lot of different things, and he was never the type to be subtle about anything. I'm sure he pissed a lot of people off over the years and it probably just caught up with him. I think the police have their work cut out for them solving this one."

"I think you're right," I said.

CHAPTER THIRTEEN
jnkdrl1

With my new haircut making me look even more like a lawman than ever, I decided to pay my first visit to Jenkins Drilling to see if I could learn anything more about Justin Ramey. I pulled off the highway and parked in front of the small brick office building that sat at the front of a huge chain-link fenced industrial yard containing drilling rigs, stacks of drilling pipe and oilfield servicing trucks. There were a few cars parked to one end of the building and I noted that one was a maroon Lincoln Navigator with personalized license plates reading *JNKDRL1.*

I asked the receptionist if I could speak to Sheryl, confessing that I didn't have an appointment and lying that Dan Cunningham had told me he was going to call ahead to let her know I was going to drop by sometime. A few minutes later a middle-aged woman with one of those bubble-shaped haircuts that were all the rage a few years ago appeared with a puzzled look on her face.

"Dan must have forgotten to tell me you were coming," she said, introducing herself.

"He may have," I said, giving her one of my business cards. "I need to talk to you about Justin Ramey."

"Oh, I see," she said, reacting like

I'd just handed her a dog turd. "Well, come on back to my office, I guess."

I followed her down a wood-paneled hallway, past the open doorway of Dallas Jenkins' large and well-appointed office. As we passed the doorway I got a glimpse of Dallas himself sitting behind a large desk with a telephone receiver pressed against his ear. He was turned in profile to the doorway and appeared to be watching the activity in the pipe yard behind the building while listening to the party on the other end of the phone line.

As we entered her office, Sheryl took her place behind her desk and offered me a chair.

"Now. How can I help you?" she said.

I explained that I was looking into the disappearance of Justin Ramey and that I was just trying to get some background about Justin's job at Jenkins Drilling.

"Well, he doesn't work here anymore," she said with raised eyebrows. "He failed to show up for work or to contact his supervisor, so we had no choice but to terminate him."

"I understand Mr. Jenkins took a special interest in Justin's job application when he was hired," I said, reading between the lines of what I'd learned over the past few days. I also hoped that my mention of Dallas Jenkins' name would send Sheryl into his office to tattle on me the minute I left. Just stirring the pot.

"I don't know anything about that," she said.

"Did Justin get his job through Field Hands?" I asked, referring to Benny Shanks' oilfield placement company.

She made the dog-turd face again.

"We don't really use Field Hands very much."

"Oh really? Why not?"

"We had some problems with some of the people they sent us. Some of them failed our random drug tests when they had supposedly been pre-screened before they were sent over here. We can't afford to take a chance on somebody being high and putting people's lives in danger out in the field."

"That is pretty disturbing," I admitted. "I thought that was one of their selling points, that they gave everybody the once-over before they recommended them to you."

"Yes sir, that's what we thought too, but it didn't turn out to be the case."

"I know it's harder than ever to keep oilfield hands that can pass a random drug test," I said.

"And, it breaks your heart when one of those tests comes back positive and it's somebody that you're friends with," she said. "I had to let an eight-year employee go just the other day because his test came back positive for methamphetamine."

"But I guess you've got to have a zero-tolerance policy where safety is concerned," I said.

"Oh, you absolutely do. And Mr. Jenkins doesn't budge an inch when it comes to making sure all our people drug-free."

"Well, I certainly have to admire a man with the courage of his convictions," I said.

CHAPTER FOURTEEN
true blue

I was sitting in my pickup watching from a block away when I saw Bob Clemmer's unmarked car pull up and park on the opposite side of the street from the scene of Benny Shanks' murder. As Clemmer got out of his car and stood in the street looking toward the crime scene, a white panel van pulled up and parked behind him. Clemmer was soon joined by a man dressed in a dark blue windbreaker with the word

"Forensics" stenciled across the back. Clemmer pointed across the street and the forensics tech took photos from several different angles before walking to the opposite gutter and retrieving the Texas Brain Freeze cup, which he placed into a plastic evidence bag.

After stowing the bag in the van, he returned with a small kit which he opened near the blue stain in the street. He spent several minutes taking samples from the stain as Clemmer looked on. Clemmer's notes on the investigation would by now have record of a follow-up visit he made to the crime scene and his discovery of the cup and memory of seeing the blue stain in the crime scene photos. The fact that the cup hadn't been discovered in the initial investigation meant that there was no way to prove it was there on the night of Benny's murder, and that it couldn't be introduced as evidence in any kind of courtroom trial. But, since it couldn't be introduced as evidence, Clemmer and I agreed that what we were doing wasn't technically the same as planting evidence. We both knew we were rationalizing our own behavior in order to get the cup tested by the crime lab. The way we saw it, worrying about what could or couldn't be used in a trial was pointless since there could be no trial at all unless there was a suspect, and at this point finding any kind of suspect was all we were concerned with.

CHAPTER FIFTEEN
expedited situation

I was sitting in a chair next to the receptionist's desk, wearing a monster truck rally t-shirt and a dirty Midland Rockhounds baseball cap as I eyed the Field Hands employment application suspiciously. Kaylee, the twentyish receptionist was beginning to lose her patience with me.

"Well, can I just fill this out and skip the signature part? Like I just sort of forgot it?" I asked.

"No, I told you already, I can't

accept it unless you sign. Why don't you want to sign it?"

I put the application down on her desk and jabbed a finger at the fine print section above the signature line.

"See that right there?" I said. "It says I'm affirming that everything on this piece of paper is true and correct."

Kaylee looked at me like she still didn't get it. I flipped the paper over.

"On this question over here about whether I could pass a drug test, you said I should just go ahead and answer yes, even though I'm not one hundred percent sure I can."

"Just go ahead and sign it and don't worry about that," she said. "You're not going to get in any trouble. It's just a formality, really."

I looked at the form some more and re-read the fine print again.

"I'm just a little worried about that test," I said. "I'm not saying I'd test positive for heroin or nothing like that, but sometimes when you're together with people on your day off and having a good time you forget they may be doing drug testing the next day at work. I always felt like my time was my own to spend any which way I wanted to."

"Then you should check the box for the Gold Expedited Processing Service," she said. "That will help with a situation like that."

I looked at the form and saw the checkbox, with an extra charge of $199 indicated next to it.

"Oh, okay," I said. "I wasn't exactly sure what *expedited* meant I guess."

"It just means we'll take care of

everything and you won't have no problems with the drug test or references or nothing like that," she said. "It's for certain situations where we need to do that."

"Well, that sounds like the way to go then," I said. "I think this is definitely an expedited situation."

"Oh, you're right," she said. "For you, it definitely is one of those."

CHAPTER SIXTEEN
tim kettle

Saturday afternoon, Angie and I had just finished a late lunch at Ribeye Ranch when I realized my suspicions about somebody following me were correct. We were coming out of the restaurant when I saw a black GMC pickup parked in a remote corner of the parking lot at the Desert Sands Motel, which was across the street from Ribeye Ranch. It was the same pickup that I had noticed a couple of blocks behind me three separate times, earlier that morning. Elmore is a small town, so it's not unusual to run across the same vehicle again and again, but I could tell from across the street that there was someone sitting in the driver's seat watching us.

After opening the passenger door for Angie, I climbed into the driver's seat and dug through the center console caddy until I found a ballpoint pen. Then, I pulled my pickup out of the Ribeye Ranch parking lot, but instead of heading back towards Angie's house, I crossed the street and pulled into the Desert Sands lot. The black pickup that had been watching us was backed into a parking place in the corner of the lot. I could see the occupant of the driver's seat sit up quickly as I drove toward him. I pulled up nose to nose, effectively blocking the black pickup in its place so that the only escape would be to back over a curb and into a xeriscaped barrier of yucca plants and pampas grass.

"What are you doing?" Angie asked, as I threw the truck in park and jotted down the black pickup's license number before stepping out of the cab.

"Wait here," I said.

I had to knock on the driver's window several times before he realized he wasn't in any immediate danger and rolled it down.

"Yeah?" he said, with a wary look in his eyes. The guy was probably in his mid-twenties and was more skilled in observing from afar than in actual confrontation.

"What's your name?" I demanded.

"Tim," he offered. I stared at him silently until the pressure was too much for him to bear.

"Tim Kettle."

I pulled out one of my business cards and held it out for him to take. He reached for it cautiously.

"Well, Tim Kettle. How about you tell whoever you're working for that it would be easier if we talked directly. I should be in my office most of the day tomorrow if he wants to drop by or call. The number's on the card."

I started to leave and then added:

"Oh, and we're going back to Miss Robbins' house now, where I picked her up earlier? I'll probably stay there for a while, maybe all night if I get lucky. Otherwise I'll be spending the night out at what used to be my folks' place. If you like, I can give you a call if I decide to go anywhere else instead."

That didn't get any response so I decided my work there was done.

"What was that all about?" Angie asked after I got back in the truck.

"Just drumming up a little business," I said.

CHAPTER SEVENTEEN
big d

"It's the God's honest truth dude," Ray said. "It was the ugliest baby I'd ever seen in my life and they just kept going on and on about how pretty it was. I was just being honest with them and all the sudden this lady's husband wants to kick my ass."

Ray had dropped by my office an hour earlier and convinced me to come next door for coffee while he ate a late breakfast at Lita's. I cut Ray's story short by standing and throwing some bills on the table, signaling him that it was time for both of us to get back to our respective occupations. Ray had been locked away in his accounting office for the first three and a half months of the year for tax season and now that business was slower he had developed a habit of spending an hour or two hanging around my office or dragging me over to Lita's to watch him eat.

I walked him outside to his vehicle while we hashed out details about where we would eat lunch later in the week. While we were standing out in front of the restaurant, Dallas Jenkins' big maroon Navigator pulled up and parked directly in front of us. Ray nodded and smiled politely at Jenkins as he exited the vehicle and stepped up onto the sidewalk, stopping there as if waiting for me and Ray to finish our conversation. Dallas Jenkins was at least six and a half feet tall and weighed probably two-fifty, but it was a muscular two-fifty. I could tell that he had probably gotten big and powerful when he was teenager and had just never let that slip away, even as he was closing in on fifty.

"Are you Buddy Griffin?" he asked, completely ignoring the fact that Ray was in the middle of telling me something about a new restaurant that had just opened up.

"Yes, I am," I said as we shook hands and he introduced himself. It was obvious he'd been a competitive hand-shaker at some point in his athletic career. Probably fit it in somewhere between football, rugby and hockey seasons.

"Have you got a few minutes to visit?" he asked, already starting toward the outside entrance to my office.

"Well, I guess I'll talk to you later," Ray offered, silently mouthing "*What the hell?*" and making a face behind Jenkins' back.

"Okay, Ray. I'll give you a call," I said, returning a shrug and then following Jenkins as he led the way into my office. The man was clearly accustomed to taking charge of the situation.

"How can I help you?" I asked, taking the power position behind my desk before he could grab it for himself.

He considered the guest chairs in front of my desk and decided to remain standing, strolling around my office and picking up things to examine them as he talked.

"My HR lady said you came by asking some questions about a former employee."

"Right," I said. "Justin Ramey. He's been missing for a couple of weeks and I'm trying to help locate him."

"Well, I just wanted to make sure there was no misunderstanding as far as his connection to Jenkins Drilling is concerned. That there is no connection anymore."

"Oh, there's no misunderstanding," I said. "I know you can't afford to keep people on the payroll if they don't show up for work when they're supposed to. I was really just trying to get some background information in case it might give me a clue where Justin might have disappeared to."

"Where he disappeared to is really not of any concern to me or my employees, Mr. Griffin. And I hope you'll quit bothering my people about this."

Judging by his attitude, Sheryl the HR lady had definitely put a bug in his ear about my implication that Dallas Jenkins had taken a special interest in the hiring of Justin Ramey.

"I apologize, sir. I really didn't mean to be a bother to your people. I know it's got to be a tremendous disappointment when you personally go out of your way to give a young man a chance and he just pisses it away like that."

"Listen, I don't know what it is you've heard, but—"

He stopped and stared at me for a few seconds.

"Are we done here?" he said finally. "Do you need anything more from us on this boy?"

"I think we're done for now," I said, holding out my hand and bracing for another encounter with his vice-like grip.

"I hope we're done *for good*," he said, with a handshake a bit softer than the one he'd given me outside. "We have young guys like this Justin come and go all the time. They're not grown up enough to hold onto a job or responsible enough to even call their boss when they're going to miss work. I wouldn't worry too much about where he is."

"Well, his wife is worried. That's why she hired me."

"Unfortunately for her, a lot of these kids look at having a wife and kids the same way they look at their job," he said. "Like they can just walk away when they get tired of them."

"Did you know Justin was Benny Shanks' nephew?" I asked as he was edging toward the door.

The proverbial deer-in-the-headlights expression was there on his face for a second, but then it was gone.

"No, I don't think I knew that," he answered, a little bit too carefully.

"It's a shame about what happened to Benny," I said. "Did you know him?"

"A little bit," he said. "Not real well. I ran into him now and then, here and there."

"Really? Justin Ramey's wife seemed to think that Benny was the one who got Justin his job working for you."

At that exact moment, Dallas Jenkins' cell phone rang loudly and he physically jerked like he'd received an electric shock. He quickly recovered, pulling the phone from its holster and pantomiming the universal 'Sorry, but I've got to take this' gesture as he stepped outside. I watched him through the glass door as he stood outside on the sidewalk listening to the party on the other end and edging toward where his Navigator was parked. I decided not to follow but instead waited to see whether he would come back inside or take the opportunity to escape further questioning.

As I expected, he chose the latter.

CHAPTER EIGHTEEN
benny's squeeze

I wandered around the showroom at Wildcatter Chevrolet for ten minutes before I finally drew the attention of someone from the sales staff. Apparently, I didn't appear sufficiently credit-worthy, or maybe I spent too much time looking at the Corvette and not enough examining the pickup at the opposite end of the room. Eventually a youngish guy wearing a purple shirt and Batman necktie tried to cozy up to me by acting like we were long lost friends. I let him rattle on a few minutes about the Car and Driver road test of the new Corvette before I asked if Madison Miller was around. He looked like I'd just insulted him and wandered off toward the maze of cubicles where he'd just come from.

Madison Miller came out a few minutes later, an attractive woman in her forties. She had frosted blonde hair and was dressed in blue jeans and low-cut blouse with lots of big silver and turquoise jewelry. Her handshake could have given Dallas Jenkins a run for his money, but she held hers a little longer and gave an extra squeeze at the end that I figured put most men in the mood to sign on the dotted line when the paperwork was presented. I gave her my business card and asked if

I could buy her a cup of coffee.

"Dinner will get you a lot further," she said with a wink. "But we can start off with coffee. You bet."

We walked across Commerce Street to The Yucca Inn, which was almost empty. I peppered her with questions about how car and truck sales were going while the waitress brought us coffee and then disappeared back into the kitchen area. When we were alone, I explained that I was looking into the disappearance of Benny Shanks' nephew.

"I understand you were friends with Benny," I said. "I'm sorry for your loss."

She smiled and watched me for a moment to see if she could read any judgment in my eyes.

"Thank you," she said quietly. "Benny and I were very close."

"Do you know Justin Ramey?" I

asked.

"I've ever met him, but Benny talked about him some. I know he worked for Benny for a while."

"Right," I said. "And, apparently Benny helped Justin get a job at Jenkins Drilling. Did you know anything about that?"

"No, but Benny didn't tell me about everything he did, so that's not unusual."

"Was Benny close to Dallas Jenkins?" I asked.

She gazed out the window and shrugged. "I don't know if you'd say they were close or not, but they were pretty well acquainted. Of course, I've known Dallas for years. Fleet sales of pickup trucks to oilfield companies is my specialty."

"Were Benny and Dallas in business together?" I asked.

She looked at me and smiled.

"Do you know much about Benny?" she asked.

"A little bit," I said. "He sold me my first beer when I was sixteen years old. And, I know he spent some time in jail over the years for some of his business enterprises."

"Then you know that people who go into business with Benny don't necessarily want it talked about openly," she said.

"I can understand that," I said. "I'm not asking for anything that might incriminate anybody, and the only reason I'm asking is that it might help me understand what was going on with Justin Ramey before he disappeared."

She took a sip of coffee and glanced out the window again before she spoke.

"Benny had something going with Dallas Jenkins, but he never told me exactly what it was. I never knew the details of what Benny was involved in when it was happening. He liked to tell me stories of things he'd done in the past, but he kept his current business to himself. It was easier for both of us that way."

"Any idea what Benny was doing over on Avenue B the night he was shot?"

"No, but like I said, he kept some things to himself."

"Did you talk to him the night he was killed?"

"No, in fact he was supposed to come over that Saturday afternoon, but he called that morning and said he wouldn't be able to make it. Said he had too many fires he was trying to put out. Or something like that."

"He was found just a few blocks from A.J.'s Lounge," I said. "What was Benny's relationship with

A.J.?"

"I heard Benny mention him a few times, but it didn't sound like they were friends. I got the idea there might have been some kind of rivalry there. Or like maybe Benny didn't like the way A.J. handled his business."

She looked out the window and took a sip of coffee before continuing.

"The stuff Benny did, the illegal stuff? It wasn't all there was to him, you know. When I got to know him, he turned out to be a really different person than I had always imagined him to be, reading about him in the paper, or listening to people gossip about what he did for a living. Knowing Benny taught me to look at people differently. Not to be so quick to judge from appearances."

"That's a powerful lesson that a

lot of people never learn," I said. "It is, isn't it?""

CHAPTER NINETEEN
deputized

Norris stood up from his desk and glanced around his office, finally pulling a *Cabela's* catalog from underneath a stack of files.

"Stand up," he said. "I don't have a bible handy, so place your right hand on this. Do you, Buddy Griffin, solemnly swear to faithfully and impartially perform all duties required of you by law and to not flash this badge around in town before you give it back?"

"I do," I said. "Do I get a gun?"

He tossed the phone book back on the desk and handed me a Starcher County Sheriff's Deputy badge.

"You already got a better gun than I could afford to issue to you. And, don't be taking any bribes while you're wearing my star."

Norris had received a call from the Loving County Sheriff's office about a cell phone found near a fire-damaged welding truck outside of Mentone, about seventy miles from Elmore. He called Norris because the numbers stored in the phone seemed to mostly be for people who lived in Elmore. When Norris figured out that one of those numbers was for the landline at Justin and Courtney Ramey's house, he asked me if I wanted to go down to Mentone to check it out since he had his plate full already. We figured if I went down there as a deputy I might have a better chance of getting the Loving County Sheriff to show me what he had, without a lot of extra explanation about who I was and why I was interested.

When I met up with Sheriff Andy Crabtree in Mentone he was in the middle of installing a TV bracket on the wall in his office but dropped what he was doing to drive me out to where they'd found the welding truck and the cell phone.

"As you can see, it was a pretty nice truck before somebody shot it up and tried to set fire to it. Didn't catch real good since the fire didn't get to the gas tank or those steel bottles behind the cab. Mostly just messed up the interior."

"Sheriff Jackson said you couldn't find a VIN number on it. Has anybody around here reported a welding truck stolen?" I asked.

"No, not around here," he said. "And the plates are from a Ford pickup from Fort Worth that the registered owner claims was traded in during that Cash For Clunkers program back in 2009. We were thinking they stole this truck somewhere else and dumped it here, then shot it full of holes. Maybe tried to set it on fire to cover up fingerprints or something. Your guess is as good as mine at this point."

"But they left the welder, tanks, bottles and hoses and tools on the truck," I said. "You'd think they'd strip that stuff off to sell if they were going to torch it."

"You'd think so," he agreed. "Whoever done this might not have been among the best and brightest of your criminal element around here."

I walked around the truck and

surveyed the damage. The windows, windshield and sides of the cab were riddled with bullet holes and decorated with the spray pattern of a shotgun load. Somebody had been really pissed off at this truck.

"Find any casings?" I asked.

"A few, of a couple of different calibers," he said. "I'm assuming they're from whoever shot the truck up, but people go hunting all over these lease properties and a casing could sit on this graded surface for a while before it got pushed down into the dirt."

"Any idea how long the truck has been here?"

"Well, the pumper who found it said he was through here a little over two weeks ago and it wasn't here then. Not much other way to put a time on when it was burned since nobody reported anything."

"What about the cell phone you mentioned to Sheriff Jackson?"

"It's back at the station and I'm just speculating as to whether it had anything to do with this truck. It was found just over there, about thirty yards to the east."

I walked over to the edge of the square graded area where the compacted chalky dirt and caliche surface gave way to low undulating dunes of red sand dotted with mesquite, scrub oak and patches of dry desert grass. The sandy soil beyond the graded square was too dry and loose to have held footprints for very long, and it had been months since the last good rain.

"Were any of the casings found over here?" I asked.

"A few, mostly by the truck though. I was thinking maybe somebody threw the phone in that direction from over here."

"I guess we're lucky they didn't shoot the phone up and then set fire to it," I said.

"Yeah, I'd sure like to do that to mine some days."

Back at his office Sheriff Crabtree handed me the phone he'd found. I recognized it as a prepaid model that could be bought and activated without requiring the user to register or sign a contract. Drug dealers were fond of using them, but so were millions of law-abiding citizens with bad credit or an aversion to long-term contractual arrangements.

"It was dead when we found it, but we had a charger that fit and it seems to be working fine now."

After scrolling through the stored phone numbers and recognizing Courtney Ramey's cell number, I went into the log of calls and saw that the last call made was to that same number on the day before Courtney Ramey told me Justin had disappeared. There were several missed calls logged beginning on the morning after Justin had disappeared.

I checked and found there were five voicemail messages waiting. The first two were from Courtney's cell, left on the Thursday morning following the disappearance, a full twenty-four hours after she had expected him home from work. The first message was short:

"Justin. It's me. Call."

Her voice didn't sound overly concerned, but carried a hint of caution, as if she were choosing her words carefully. Her second call was made two hours later:

"Justin, call me. Please. I need to know what's going on and that you're okay."

The third call had come that Thursday night and was from an unidentified number. The message contained several seconds of silence with the background noise a mixture of muffled voices, laughter and music. The fourth message was left early Friday morning from the same number. I immediately recognized the voice of Benny Shanks:

"Justin. Boy, where are you? I need to hear from you ASAP or the shit's gonna hit the fan."

The fifth message was left at a little after nine o'clock on Friday morning, from Courtney's cell number again, with the sound of children yelling in the background.

"It's me," she said. "Call me if you can."

I turned to Sheriff Crabtree.

"Can I take this with me?" I asked, holding up the phone.

"Sure thing. Norris thought you'd want to. Let me get the paperwork and you can sign for it."

"What are you going to do about the truck?" I asked.

"We'll get somebody to tow it to the county impound yard when we can, but the wrecker we usually use is out of town and won't be back until next week."

"Do you mind if I bring somebody down here to look at it again?"

"Think you got somebody can ID the thing?"

"Maybe," I said. "At least give us an idea who may have built the welding bed."

"Bring 'em on down anytime. Call me ahead of time and I'll buy you lunch."

"Oh, I don't want to take up any more of your time. We'll just take a quick look on our own and stay out of your hair. I'll let you know if he comes up with anything that might help with your investigation."

"Well, suit yourself. You're welcome down here anytime."

CHAPTER TWENTY
c.d.l.

On the drive back to Elmore I thought about the contents of Justin Ramey's cell phone messages and what they might tell me about what he had been up to before he disappeared. When Courtney Ramey had come to see me, she told me that the drilling rig that Justin and the Jenkins Drilling crew were working on that day was located near Eunice, New Mexico which was due northwest of Elmore. The area outside Mentone where the cell phone had been found was southwest of Elmore, and about fifty miles south of Eunice. For somebody to pass through Mentone when driving between Elmore and Eunice would mean driving eighty or more miles out of the way on what would have otherwise been a trip of about fifty miles. It didn't make sense. Most oilfield workers drove the shortest distance possible to and from the rig and generally at speeds well in excess of the posted limits.

Another thing that bothered me was why Courtney Ramey hadn't left her first message for Justin until a full day after she had expected him home from his Tuesday to Wednesday overnight shift. Of course, if Justin were a rarity for his generation and seldom used his cell phone, then Courtney may have assumed it would be turned off.

The fact that Benny Shanks was looking for him just twenty-four hours before he was murdered made me think that Justin was involved in something that might be tied to what happened to Benny.

I didn't know what to think about the shot-up and abandoned welding truck and whether it was related to Justin's disappearance, but it was another coincidence that was too big to ignore. And the fact that it was fitted with stolen license plates and had no easily-found VIN number added to my suspicions that there was more to the story than a stolen and abandoned vehicle.

When I got back to Elmore, I went back to my office to check my messages and make a few phone calls. I ordered a cheese enchilada plate from next door and carried it back to my desk. The phone rang before I could take my first bite.

"Did you arrest anybody down there?" It was Norris.

"No, but I did get into a shootout and accidentally killed a couple head of cattle."

"Was there anything worth seeing?"

"He let me bring the phone back with me and I got to see a burned-out welding truck with about a hundred bullet holes in it."

"He was telling me about that. What was that about, do you think?"

"I don't know. I'm gonna take a welder buddy of mine down there to look at it. See if maybe he can recognize who it belonged to."

"That's a good idea. I bet all them welders know each other. Borrow welding rods from each other when they run out and stuff like that," he said.

"That's what I was thinking. Plus, I get to drive around some more and act like a deputy."

"Did I explain that we don't reimburse for mileage?"

"What about for uniform cleaning?"

"Next, you'll want us to issue you a uniform. Hey, I got another call coming in. Let me know if I can help."

As I ate I wondered what would happen with Norris and whether he would be able to keep his job once it became known that he had owed significant gambling debts to Benny Shanks. So much of what lay ahead for him would depend on politics, and I really didn't have a good feel for the players in the Starcher County political arena and how Norris fit in among them. I had avoided spending much time thinking about what he'd told me, and I knew that it was because I was disappointed that he'd allowed himself to get caught up in such a mess. Of course, if Benny Shanks' murder was solved quickly, or at least a suspect identified, there would be less chance someone might speculate that Norris had been involved somehow. The best thing I could do for Norris as a friend was to keep digging into Justin Ramey's actions in the hope that it would shed some light on who killed Benny.

Being careful not to talk with my mouth full, I called Jenkins Drilling and asked to speak to Sheryl, the Human Resources person. She sounded cheerful and professional when she answered, but her tone changed when she learned it was me calling.

"Oh," she said. "What do you need?"

"I'm sorry to bother you again, but I was wondering if you could tell me if Justin Ramey had his CDL?"

CDL was shorthand for commercial driver's license, a certification required for anyone who drove a commercial vehicle, like any of the vehicles owned by Jenkins Drilling.

There was a pause on the other end of the line, followed by an audible sigh.

"Hold on, let me pull his file."

I managed to get in a few bites before she returned. The refried beans were especially good today, probably the result of an extra smidgen of lard in the recipe.

"Justin Ramey does have his CDL," she said when she picked up the line again.

"Thank you so much for that," I said. "I'm curious. Does Jenkins Drilling employ any welders?"

Another pause.

"Are you asking because it relates to Justin Ramey, or is there some other reason?"

"Oh, I was just wondering. I figured you might need one now and then to do repairs to your rigs and I've got a welder friend looking for work."

"Well, your friend is certainly welcome to come by and fill out a job application. We do have a couple of welders on our payroll currently, but there may be openings in the future."

"I'll tell him that. Sheryl, I sure do appreciate all the help you've given me. I'll try not to bother you again."

"Oh, you're no bother," she said, although not very convincingly.

CHAPTER TWENTY-ONE
no beans

"What do you think?" she said.

"Too much tomato flavor and not enough chile powder," I said, dropping the Styrofoam bowls in a trash barrel.

Angie and I had just finished our second sample-sized bowl of chili at the Elmore United Way Chili Cookoff. There were at least two-dozen temporary booths set up on the courthouse lawn, mostly sponsored by local businesses and staffed by their employees. There were a few outsiders who traveled the chili-cookoff circuit and towed their custom-made grill setups behind dually pickups.

"What about the beans?" she asked

"I don't have a strict no-beans policy," I said. "I do admit that in some cases, beans can enhance the chili experience."

"And extend it, too," she laughed.

"Well, I wasn't going to bring that part up. At least not right away," I said. "Although, I know it might come up later."

We had made most of the circuit of booths, intending to sample a few and then go back to our favorite for a bigger bowl. Jenkins Drilling was sponsoring a booth at the edge of the lawn and had brought in a large barbecue pit trailer where they were cooking and smoking various meats in addition to chili. We stopped at their booth and got a chili sampler and smoked brisket burrito and strolled toward an empty shaded bench as we traded bites.

"How's your investigation going?" she asked.

We hadn't talked much about Justin Ramey's disappearance or Benny's shooting, and I hadn't revealed where I had been sticking my nose in order to investigate both events. I knew that if I brought it up I would have to mention Dallas Jenkins, and I knew she was sensitive to discussing rumors about him since he was a good client of the Donnelly Law Firm.

"Oh, it's going okay," I said, treading lightly. "I'm still just trying to figure out if this Justin kid going missing might be related to Benny Shanks getting shot. Might just be a coincidence that he's Benny's nephew, or there might be something there."

"You mentioned before that he disappeared about the same time that Benny got shot."

"A few days before," I said. I started to say more, but then stopped.

"What?" she said.

"Nothing. It's just that we probably shouldn't get into it right now," I said.

"Because?"

"Because Justin Ramey was working for Jenkins Drilling at the time of his disappearance."

"Well? What's—Oh, the other night. The talk about Dallas Jenkins. I'm sorry, I should apologize for how I acted."

"No, it's no problem," I said. "I understand your position—"

"No, I've thought about it a lot,"

she said. "And, it wasn't the first time I've heard rumors about him. So, go ahead. I promise not to burst into tears."

I started from the beginning, telling her about Courtney Ramey appearing in my office a week after Justin disappeared, and three days after Benny's murder.

"Hold on," she said. "She waits a full week before she starts trying to get help? What's up with that?"

"Well, she said she had reported it to the police, but she wasn't getting enough of a response from them, so she came to me. Justin's apparently been in trouble with the law before."

"But, he disappeared what, about four days before Benny was shot?"

"Yeah. If it had been the same night, or closer to the time of the shooting, I'd be more certain about there being some connection. As it is, I'm just not convinced the two things are related."

"And, you said he works for Jenkins Drilling?"

"He did, until they fired him for not showing up. I'm not getting a lot of cooperation from them. Courtney told me that Justin was supposed to be picked up at their trailer by his crew boss on Tuesday afternoon, but the crew boss won't admit to it. He says Justin missed work and the Company fired him, which is what the woman in HR confirms. A neighbor lady told me that sometimes Justin got picked up for work by a white crew-cab pickup and sometimes by a big maroon SUV with personalized plates, which fits the description of Dallas Jenkins' vehicle. Nobody seems to know who Justin left the trailer with that Tuesday, because Courtney was gone and the neighbor didn't see."

"I think Jenkins Drilling may have more than one of those maroon SUV's," she said.

"Good to know," I said.

I told her about the burned-out bullet hole-ridden welding truck with Justin Ramey's cell phone found nearby.

"Bullet holes? That's kind of scary. Unless they got there after it was abandoned. Maybe somebody using it for target practice?"

"I don't know," I said. "Pumpers drive those roads pretty regularly, so I don't think it was out there long before it got reported."

"And Justin's phone was found nearby," she said, repeating what I'd told her. "What do you think he was doing out there?"

"No idea. At first, I thought maybe he tried to get a ride to the rig he was working on with a welder, but the truck was found too far away and in a different direction from Elmore for that to make any sense. And, the fact that they haven't been able to identify who owned the truck doesn't help."

I described the call history and messages left on Justin's phone and how the missed calls and messages had stopped on Friday morning.

"So, do you think Courtney and Benny got in touch with Justin some other way, so they quit calling?"

"Must have. Either that or there was some other reason that made them stop calling Justin's cell."

"But then Courtney comes into your office what, four days later to ask for help finding Justin? That wouldn't make sense if she heard from him on Friday."

"No, but nothing else about this makes much sense," I said. "Like the fact that Benny apparently helped Justin get hired on at Jenkins Drilling, but I never was able to get Dallas Jenkins to admit any involvement in giving Justin his job, or that he even knew Benny was Justin's uncle."

"Understand I'm not trying to defend Dallas Jenkins, but maybe somebody else at Jenkins Drilling hired Justin," she said.

"That might explain it," I said. "But Dallas just seems like such a hands-on type of business owner that I would think he has a good handle on who they've got on the payroll."

I related Clemmer's request for help on the Benny Shanks murder but didn't mention anything to her about Norris' gambling debt to

Benny.

"Have you got time to do that while you're looking for Justin?" she asked.

"I think so. I'm hoping that digging into Benny's murder might actually lead to something that can help me find out what happened to Justin."

"Okay but be careful. If you end up solving both cases Clemmer may get you an office in the police headquarters."

"Oh, don't worry. I refuse to man a desk anywhere I can't have an enchilada plate with rice and beans delivered to my desk."

"There you go with those beans again," she said.

CHAPTER TWENTY-TWO
side gig

There was an older model Toyota parked behind the Ramey's pickup and I could hear the screaming voices of several children arguing when I knocked on the door of their mobile home. Courtney's sister was there for the afternoon and had brought three kids of her own with her. There seemed to be some type of yelling competition taking place among the kids, so we stepped outside to talk. I told her that Justin's cell phone had been found and described where.

"Do you have any idea why his phone would be found so far away from where he was supposed to be working that day?"

She slowly shook her head. "No, not unless somebody ripped it off or something."

"Somebody also tried to torch a vehicle nearby. A welding truck."

"A welding truck?"

"Like a welder would drive. With a bunch of bullet holes in it. Looked like somebody tried to set it on fire but it didn't catch completely."

"Oh my God, are you serious?"

She sat down on a weathered aluminum lawn chair and then immediately stood up again.

"Where did you say this was again?"

"Just outside of Mentone, a little ways off the highway on a lease location."

"Oh, my God."

"Courtney, is there something you haven't told me about Justin's disappearance?"

She didn't answer, just stood looking down at the dirt, shaking her head and reaching up to tuck her hair behind her ears every few seconds.

"If there's more that you need to tell me, now would be the time to do it. Justin had something to do with that welding truck, didn't he?"

She started sobbing quietly.

"I told him it was too good to be true," she said, sniffling and wiping away tears with the heels of her hands. "I knew there was no way somebody would pay him that much just to drive a truck unless there was something illegal or dangerous about it."

"Who was paying him?"

"I don't know. Justin never would answer when I asked him. It was all in cash and off the books, and a lot more money than he makes on the days he works on the rigs."

"He does both?"

"Most of the time he works on Dan Cunningham's crew. But sometimes he would get a call telling him they wanted him to deliver a truck to Van Horn and drive a different truck back here."

"Were these welding trucks?"

She looked up and nodded, her eyes bloodshot and brimming.

"Always. He drives one welding truck down there and another welding truck back."

"What does he do when he gets there?"

"He just drives to an empty lot in Van Horn. There's always another welding truck and driver waiting. They trade keys and Justin gets in the other truck and drives it back here."

"Was he scheduled to drive the night he disappeared?"

"Yeah, he was. He always tells me so I know I won't be able to reach him on his phone. He's not supposed to even take a phone with him, but after he figured out they weren't going to check each time he decided to start carrying his. You know, just in case something happened," she said, beginning to sob harder.

I gave her a few seconds.

"Did Dan Cunningham know that Justin wasn't going to meet the rest of the crew at the rig that night?"

"I don't know," she sniffled. "I'm not sure if Dan knows about the other job or not."

"So, somebody else besides Dan picked Justin up here on the days he was going to make one of those runs."

She nodded. "Yeah, I never knew who it was."

She reached up and wiped her tears away again and looked at me.

"This don't look good, does it?" she said.

"To be honest with you," I said. "No, it doesn't."

Mark Cotton

CHAPTER TWENTY-THREE
big d again

Tuesday night was when they served Mexican food at the Elmore Country Club, so Angie and I were sitting in the big dining room that overlooked the practice putting green. I wasn't a member at the Country Club, but they'd begun opening their dining room to the public when the big oil companies moved their offices out of town and company-paid memberships dwindled.

I was just finishing a cup of cream

of jalapeno soup when Dallas Jenkins, along with two other men, walked past our table on their way to the exit.

"Well, hello counselor," he boomed at Angie in his well-practiced attention-getting voice as he paused at our table. "How are things in the legal world?"

"Going well, Dallas," she said. "Have you met Buddy Griffin?"

"Why yes, I have," he said, without making any move to offer one of his bone-crunching handshakes. "Good to see you again, Buddy. As a matter of fact, can we speak privately? Miss Robbins, I'm sorry to interrupt. Do you mind if I drag him away for a second?"

"Not at all," she said, glancing at me with a hint of apprehension in her eyes.

Jenkins told the men he was with

that he'd meet them outside and then began walking ahead of me toward the small bar area off the dining room. I followed, feeling somewhat like I was being led to the Principal's office while my classmates watched. The bar was empty and once inside the doorway Jenkins spun around and faced me with his hands on his hips.

"I thought we agreed you wouldn't go bothering my people anymore about this Ramey kid," he said, his face growing red and his breathing letting me know that he'd rather we were out in the parking lot where he could take a swing at me.

"Oh, you mean my phone call to Sheryl the other day? I apologize. Maybe I should have called you directly. There was a welding truck found down around Mentone that I think might be related to Justin's disappearance. Are you missing a welding truck?"

"A welding truck?" he said, just to give me some kind of response while he tried to decide whether to tell the truth or not.

"Yeah," I said. "Looked like it might have been a pretty nice one until somebody shot it full of holes and tried to set it on fire."

His threatening posture relaxed somewhat as he considered what I'd said.

"Where's Justin?" I asked.

He looked at me quickly.

"Listen, don't you even think for a minute I know anything about where he is. I've told you we've helped you all we can help you. Now, if you'll excuse me I've got people waiting for me outside."

"You know this is gonna come back and bite you on the ass, don't you?" I said as he walked away. I didn't have a clue exactly what it was that was going to come back and bite him on the ass, but I knew he was scrambling to hide something about Justin's welding truck run, and that particular something was probably the reason Justin Ramey hadn't come home when he was supposed to.

Jenkins stopped in his tracks and started to turn around, but then continued on out the door.

CHAPTER TWENTY-FOUR
welding truck

The next morning, I was sitting alone in a booth at The Yucca Inn when a rough-looking biker type walked in and sat down across from me. He was at least six-foot-five and wide enough to take up most of his side of the booth.

"What do you say we go play some nine-ball?" he said with a fearsome grin. "You win and you can go by my house and load my scooter in the back of that shiny pickup of yours and drive away."

"And if I don't win?" I asked.

He grinned even bigger and laughed.

"Oh, you don't want to even think about not winning. It won't be pretty."

"How many balls you gonna spot me?" I asked.

"Spot you? What the hell are you talking about? I heard you spend all your free time playing pool down at the Senior Citizens Center and taking old people's Social Security checks."

"Thanks for meeting me," I said as we shook hands.

Myron "Mad Dog" Fulton, in contrast to his outward appearance, was one of the nicest people I had met since my return to Elmore. He was a hard-working family man who just happened to love motorcycles and the biker lifestyle. He also knew just about everything there was to know about welding and was familiar with most of the welders working around the Permian Basin.

"So, let's go look at this welding truck," he said.

I left my pickup at The Yucca Inn and rode with Mad Dog in a monster of a truck with dual rear wheels, a massive welding unit and the logo of Wild West Welding painted on the doors. Mad Dog worked at Wild West during the week and spent most of his free time on his motorcycle. On the ride to Mentone we listened to a classic rock station on the radio and talked about some of Mad Dog's biker friends that I had met a few months earlier while working another case. I had decided to drive directly to the location of the abandoned welding truck to take a look on our own rather than contacting Sheriff Crabtree to meet us. If Mad Dog couldn't tell me anything new by looking then there was no reason to involve anybody else.

"Well, they sure did a job on it, didn't they?" Mad Dog asked as he parked and began walking around the truck.

"Do you recognize who it might belong to?" I asked

"No, it's a little different design than I've seen around here," he said. "Every welder has different ideas about how they want the bed of their truck built, and a lot of them build their bed themselves and put their own personality into them. That's why sometimes you'll see welding beds made with tail-lights salvaged from old wrecked cars or with toolboxes built in. This one's got a little longer bed than some others do."

He continued walking around the truck in circles, stopping to give a closer examination to several different areas, pulling a tape measure from his pocket and making some measurements, then retrieving a large flashlight from his own truck before dropping to the ground and crawling underneath the burned-out truck on his back. When he came out his jeans and denim work shirt were covered with the fine white dirt of the crushed caliche that had been hauled in to make the drilling location.

"Any ideas?" I asked.

He stood looking at the truck as he slapped at the dust on his clothes.

"There's a couple of things that seem kind of strange," he said. "Come over here and look at this. See how nice these welds are here? Somebody took a lot of time when they were building this to make sure they got good welds and cleaned off any excess metal, ground it down real nice and smooth, like that, see?"

He dropped back down to the ground at the back end of the welding bed. I knelt and watched as he directed the beam of the flashlight at the underneath side of the welding bed.

"Now, if you look under here you can see these two places, right here, where these two plates have been welded on. See how those welds are rougher and they didn't try to finish them off at all? Pretty sloppy work. They were painted black like the rest of the bed but look at how easily the paint scrapes off. Those plates were welded on and the welds were done later, then sprayed with a different kind of black paint. The rest of the bed was painted professionally, but not where those plates were added. I'd say the welds right there were made later and painted with a can of spray paint like you'd buy at the hardware store. And, judging by how soft the paint is, I'd say the paint job was pretty recent. Then after that, somebody cut right through the middle of the plates with a steel saw."

He played the beam of his flashlight along the dirt underneath the truck.

"And, see how that metal dust on the ground underneath the truck reflects the light? It looks like they cut through those plates while the truck was parked right here."

"Why would they cut through them?" I asked.

"See how the plates are welded

across that gap that runs along there?" he asked. "Now, if you follow that gap you'll see it runs all around the outside of the bed. Now, look at the top side of the bed as a whole and you'll see it's built like a big flat upside-down box. You see that?"

"Yeah," I said, walking around and looking at the top of the bed and then bending to see the gap that ran all the way around it. "It's like they built the top part separately and set it down on top of what, a smaller box or platform of some kind?"

"Now, come up here and look at this," he said, scrambling to his feet and moving to the front of the bed, where he dropped to the ground and slithered underneath the truck.

I went around to the other side and joined him on the ground. He shone the beam of the flashlight up into a wide gap between the welding bed and the back of the cab.

"See the way the surface of the metal is uneven right there, and there?"

"Yeah. What does that mean?"

"It means there's been some welding done on the other side of the metal that's showing. When you weld two pieces of metal together you get them both hot enough to melt so they can be fused together. If the metal gets hot enough you can see where its fused even from the other side. "

"So, what's welded to the other side in those two places? Some kind of braces?"

"Could be, but I think they're hinges."

"Hinges?"

"Yessir. I think there's two hinges

welded on the other side of the surface you're looking at. That's what it looks like to me, with there being two areas like that and positioned the way they are."

"Why would there be hinges placed there?" I asked.

"I don't know, but I've got a hunch."

"Hey, hunches are my bread and butter," I said. "Lay it on me."

"Okay, we've got those welded on plates I showed you at the back that are there to hold the upside-down box of the welding bed to the platform that's underneath it, right?"

"Gotcha."

"And, we've got what I think are two hinges at the front of the welding bed, just behind the welding unit."

"Okay."

"Now, see the bottom of the

platform here?" he said playing the beam of the flashlight along the underside of the smaller platform that sat inside the upside-down box that was the top surface of the welding bed.

"Yeah?" I said.

"Well when I measured a few minutes ago, I found that there's about ten inches distance from this underside of the platform to the top side of the welding bed."

"So, there's some dead space between the bottom and the top surfaces of the welding bed?"

"Exactly. A *lot* of dead space. And, if you were going to build a welding bed with that much dead space, it would make sense only if you were going to utilize the space somehow, by building in some tool boxes or storage areas, maybe openings to store lengths of steel tubing or rods. And, this bed doesn't have anything like that."

"Just a big flat sealed dead space," I said.

"Right."

"Like a big metal storage locker, with a hinged top," I said.

"Yep, pretty much."

"But the top would have to weigh quite a bit wouldn't it?"

He shrugged. "Sure, but all you need is a shop crane to lift it. Pretty easy to find one of those in any oilfield shop around here. A portable crane would work too, and there's plenty of those used in the oilfield. The crane on my truck would lift it with no problem."

"You think it would?" I asked.

"One way to find out."

I called Sheriff Crabtree while Mad Dog backed his truck up to the rear of the burned-out truck and positioned the tall 'A' frame of the truck's gin poles above its bed. A thick steel cable ran from the winch mounted on the back of Mad Dog's truck, up to a pulley where the gin poles met and then down to a heavy steel hook that Mad Dog fastened to the welding bed. I told Crabtree what we had in mind and got his blessing on what we were going to do. Then I asked if he'd mind being present when Mad Dog attempted to open the bed. His cruiser rolled up in a cloud of dust a few minutes later. We gave Mad Dog the go-ahead and watched him work as I filled Crabtree in on Mad Dog's theory. After double-checking his rig's setup, Mad Dog hit the power switch and the motor began to whine, pulling the back end of the welding bed up at an angle, like the lid on a cigar box. He kept at it until he had raised the back edge of the bed surface up about four feet, and then stopped with it hanging there.

I stepped closer and looked under the now-angled bed surface at the open chamber beneath it.

"Well, it was a good theory, anyway," Sheriff Crabtree said.

The hidden compartment was empty except for some traces of dust that Crabtree decided looked suspicious enough to test.

Mad Dog and I waited while Crabtree went to his cruiser for a narcotics field test kit.

"I guess your gut was right," I said.

"Just an educated guess."

"Any educated guesses about who might have built this?"

"Not right offhand. Anybody who built it knew exactly why they were building it though. It's a pretty well-thought-out design for concealing that compartment."

Sheriff Crabtree's field tests didn't

reveal any evidence of drugs inside the compartment. The dust was apparently just plain old dirt. But, neither of us were very surprised the tests didn't give a positive result.

"It wouldn't have made much sense for somebody to go to so much trouble to conceal something and then get sloppy with the packaging," Crabtree said. "They wouldn't want a drug dog giving away their hiding place."

Once Crabtree made some photographs he let Mad Dog lower the bed and Mad Dog and I started the drive back to Elmore. I waited until we'd talked over the drug trafficking angle for a while and moved on to sports before I brought up Jenkins Drilling.

"You know any welders that work for Jenkins Drilling?" I asked.

"I think they've got a couple over

there right now," he said. "I don't really know them very well. One of them is pretty young and can't weld worth a shit. The other guy's pretty good though. I think I heard he learned to weld when he was in prison down in south Texas somewhere."

"That's interesting," I said.

"Yeah," he said. "I guess it's not a bad trade to learn if you can get somebody to hire you when you get out."

"Sounds like he didn't have a problem getting Dallas Jenkins to hire him."

CHAPTER TWENTY-FIVE
d.e.a.

Two days later, I was standing at my office door watching an empty plastic grocery bag and a tumbleweed race each other down the middle of the street when my phone rang. The grocery bag seemed to be winning, so I pulled my attention away long enough to answer. It was Shane Gerber, a DEA agent from El Paso. He'd heard about the welding truck from Sheriff Crabtree and wanted to know if I'd learned anything new.

"No," I said. "You got any ideas?"

"Well, I might, but what exactly is your role there? I called the Starcher County Sheriff's Office and they said I was confused if I thought you were a Deputy there."

I filled him in on my law enforcement background and explained that I was working for Norris in an unofficial capacity pending an increase in his staffing budget. This seemed to ease his concern.

Gerber told me he thought the welding truck I had gone to look at might be related to a turf war between the Juarez and Sinaloa drug cartels.

"Have you seen the truck?" I asked.

"No, but Crabtree sent me some pictures of it he took when you had the back end opened up. Pretty clever design."

"To a point," I said. "But if my welder buddy figured it out so quickly, would it really stand up to much scrutiny at a border checkpoint?"

"Probably not," Gerber admitted. "My guess is they get waved through the checkpoint by somebody on the cartel's payroll."

"It's what, a couple hundred miles from where the truck was found to Juarez? Does that mean we're talking about the Juarez Cartel?"

"Not necessarily," Gerber said. "Could be Sinaloa just as easily. Just when we think we've got their organizational structure and turf pinned down it all changes, and Sinaloa has been moving in to take over territory that the Juarez Cartel has been in control of. And then you've also got free agents whose alliances shift back and forth between the Sinaloa, Juarez, Los

Zetas organizations."

I filled him in on Justin Ramey's disappearance and Benny Shanks' subsequent murder and told him I thought they were probably both related to the welding truck somehow.

"Probably so," he said. "Most of the violence happens on the other side of the border, but sometimes it does spill over. I'll be getting with Clemmer at the Elmore PD to get what they've got on the Shanks murder, but if you find anything else that indicates a link to that truck, I'd appreciate a heads-up."

CHAPTER TWENTY-SIX
folding

When I had come back to Elmore after leaving Austin, I moved into the house where I was raised and where my parents had accumulated rooms full of personal belongings over decades. I was slowly working my way through those rooms, giving away what could be used by charities around town and hauling off what couldn't. The house was five miles outside of town and sat a couple hundred yards off of the highway, so it was quiet and peaceful most of the time. And, being isolated like it was I rarely had to answer the door unless it was for an invited guest.

I was folding laundry on the kitchen table with Joe Ely's first album playing on my parent's old console stereo when the doorbell rang. Normally, I would have heard any car that approached the house, but I had been singing along to *Boxcars* while trying to match up socks, so the doorbell caught me by surprise. Cleve Campbell stood on the front porch, wearing a suit that probably cost more than my entire wardrobe and flanked by two young black men who looked like they'd spent some time playing college ball.

After introductions, I invited the three of them inside. Campbell ordered the two other men to wait on the porch and followed me into the den.

"I hope you don't mind my coming to see you at your home," he began. "The press seems to want to write a story every time I show up in public these days and, well I just wanted to talk to you without a lot of people wondering what it might be about. I'm sure you can understand."

"Of course," I said, wondering to myself if there had ever been a time when Cleve Campbell had been less than delighted to see his name in print. "What can I do for you?"

"It's a rather delicate matter, Mr. Griffin," he said, lowering his voice in case either of the two guys outside had their ear pressed against the door or somebody from the Elmore Sentinel had the house bugged.

"As you may be aware, I am a candidate to represent this district in the Texas House of Representatives."

"I think I've seen your name in the papers," I said.

"You've probably also seen that I've been speaking up on behalf of those who were gunned down by the police at a local nightclub a while back."

I held up a hand to stop him.

"Just as an aside here, Mr. Campbell, let me mention that I'm a former police officer myself and I'm not absolutely sure that the term *gunned down by the police* is the best description for what happened in this particular situation. Just based on what I've heard."

"Fair enough," he said. "And, yes I do know you're a former police officer. I have a lot of connections in Austin and I made some inquiries about you before I decided to come here. You'll be happy to know your reputation is spotless among those I talked to."

I smiled politely and tried to contain my delight, gesturing for him to continue.

"I think we can both agree that what happened at the nightclub was unfortunate," he said. "And the only reason I'm here in Elmore, as someone who understands the workings of the political system, is to be there to represent the side of those who might not otherwise be represented. But, for me to properly represent those people, it's important for me to understand all of the factors in play."

"What kind of factors?" I asked.

"Oh, all sorts of factors, such as – may I speak frankly?"

"Of course, you may. We're just

a couple of guys sitting around shooting the shit."

He chuckled at that.

"You know, Mr. Griffin. I didn't build the most successful African-American run company in Texas by being a poor judge of character. I did it by weeding out liars and cheats anytime I found them within the ranks of my company, and by refusing to do business with that type of people whenever I encountered them. And, I've got to confess that I rarely give anybody the benefit of the doubt. Over the years, if somebody looked dirty or dishonest to me they were gone, no questions asked and no excuses accepted."

"That policy seems to have worked out for you," I said, giving his ego a subtle stroke.

"It did. I may have missed some opportunities as a result or failed to give an otherwise valuable employee the shot they deserved, but it served me well in building my company. Unfortunately, when I entered the political arena I discovered that the same restrictive viewpoint just doesn't play well. A certain amount of flexibility seems to be the key to long-range success as a politician."

"I wouldn't disagree with that, from what I've observed," I said.

"And so, I find myself in a situation where I've publicly taken the position of defending of the rights of the patrons of A.J.'s Lounge, even though I might not personally condone the behavior of those patrons while gathered there. And, in the time that has passed since I took that position, events have transpired and information has come to light that make me start to question whether it was wise to interject myself into this situation."

"What has you concerned?" I asked, as if I hadn't already put two and two together.

"For one, the murder of Benny Shanks, a purported local crime figure, so close in proximity to A.J.'s Lounge. Add to that rumors we've heard about the possible involvement of A.J. Lipscomb in local drug trafficking and a possible partnership with Benny Shanks."

"You're worried the blowback might end up hurting your campaign."

"Exactly. So, you can see why I have a keen interest in learning who may have been involved in what happened to Mr. Shanks. Plus, the longer this crime goes unsolved the more likely the police will try to pin it on the first black man they happen to arrest for any other reason."

"How does that involve me?"

"I've got eyes and ears all over this town, and I know you've been asking around about Benny Shanks' murder. And, I gather that you're doing so with the blessings of the Elmore Police Department. I came here today to open a dialog in the hope that you will keep me informed about your progress on the investigation."

"On what basis?"

"On the basis that I represent the African American community here, and I need to look out for their interests in this situation."

"Huh," I said. "I wasn't aware you had an official role here."

"Well, not official, no," he said.

"No, you're down here because you—"

I stopped myself before finishing.

"I'm kind of busy right now," I

said. "Why don't you just leave me your card and I'll be in touch if I have anything to report."

I still had half a basket of laundry to finish folding, and one lonely sock whose mate seemed to have vanished into thin air..

CHAPTER TWENTY-SEVEN
date night

"I can't believe you actually take the pickles off a hamburger before eating it," I said.

"And, I can't believe you actually order additional pickles. One or two is plenty. More than plenty, actually."

Angie and I were in my pickup, parked in a space at Flat-Top's Drive-In, a fast-food place where you ordered your meal using an intercom system and teenaged waitresses on roller skates delivered it to your car. It was a throwback to the drive-in diners of decades past, and the weather was so nice we decided to give the burgers a try.

While we ate, I caught Angie up on the latest developments in my investigations into Benny Shanks murder and Justin Ramey's disappearance.

"Do you think Justin is still alive?" she asked.

"I don't know what to think. If Courtney knows he's still alive she sure wouldn't admit to it. I've got to think he would have phoned her by now if he was. But, maybe they've been in touch and she's just hiding it, the same way she hid the fact that Justin was getting paid in cash to drive a truck that may or may not have been transporting something illegal."

"Do you think that's what was

going on?" she asked.

"I've got a pretty good hunch there were drugs involved. Mad Dog showed me where they sawed through the welds to open the back of that truck while it was parked out there in the middle of nowhere. Not much reason to do that unless there was something valuable hidden inside."

"And, Courtney wasn't any help in figuring out who picked Justin up in the maroon SUV on the nights he didn't work on the rig?" she asked.

"No, or if she knew she wasn't ready to tell me yet. You were right though, Jenkins Drilling has at least four different maroon SUV's that I've seen parked at their offices at various times."

"What about Benny Shanks' murder. You making any progress on that one?"

I told her about the blue stain in

the street next to Benny's car and the Texas Brain Freeze cup that Cuatro had presented to me.

"Well, that could be something, couldn't it?" she asked.

"Could be. It may take a while for the State Crime Lab to get back to us though. And, I'm not really sure how much help it can be."

CHAPTER TWENTY-EIGHT
big d little t

The thing I always liked about investigative police work was that just when I was beginning to think I had something figured out, some new piece of information would fall in my lap and prove me completely wrong.   Even though I wasn't carrying a badge anymore, or filling out forms in triplicate to record my every move, as a private detective I was still doing basic investigative police work. And, new information could still knock down even the most solid of my theories when I least expected it. That's why I was a little taken aback when Dallas Jenkins walked into my office and sat down in front of my desk, looking like a man with nowhere else to turn.

"I think need your help," he said. "I think I need to hire you."

"What do you think you need to hire me to do?" I said.

He looked around, shook his head and leaned forward and stared at the floor.

"Do you have kids?" he asked.

"I've got a daughter," I said.

When he looked up his eyes were worried. He blew out a nervous breath and leaned back in his chair.

"It's my son Trey," he said. "He works in the business. He's my operations manager. He's a good kid, really. Kid. Hell, he's thirty-two. But, he still acts like a kid sometimes, some of the shit he pulls."

"Gets into some mischief?" I asked.

"Oh, more than mischief," he answered. "I've been bailing that little sonofabitch's ass out of trouble since he was twelve. I thought he had straightened up the last couple of years though. Thought we'd finally gotten past all that."

He shook his head and stared at the wall and I could see his anger building.

"He's in trouble again?"

"Yeah, I think so," he said. Quiet. Almost resigned. "I think it may be something illegal."

He looked up at me.

"How does that work? I mean I know you used to be a cop and all that before you came back to town, but does it work kind of like that lawyer-client privilege deal if I talk to you about something?"

I nodded slowly.

"To a certain extent," I said. "Why don't you tell me a little about what's going on and I'll stop you if it sounds like you might want to bring an attorney into the picture."

"Well, I started to go to my lawyer first, but I thought you might know your way around this type of situation a little better than him, and I know you've already been looking into trying to find Justin Ramey."

"This is related to Justin's disappearance?"

"It is. And I'm sorry I acted like such an asshole before, but I really didn't know anything about where he might be until Trey told me a little about what was going on this morning on the phone."

He looked quickly at the door leading into Lita's Little Mexico and then glanced at the other door leading to the street.

"I need to you keep this completely confidential," he said, leaning forward and lowering his voice. "Trey got himself mixed up in some kind of deal where he was acting as a go-between in an illegal transaction. To tell you the truth, he was helping these fellas to transport some drugs. I don't know all the details yet but something went wrong along the way and now there's people coming around looking for Trey and he's scared for his life."

"Has anybody threatened him?"

"Not directly, but here's the other part; his partner in this deal was Benny Shanks. And I guess you know what happened to him a couple of weeks ago."

"Does Trey know who shot Benny?" I asked.

"No, but he's pretty sure it has something to do with this deal that went bad."

"Does he think whoever shot Benny might be coming after him next?"

"He was scared enough that he left town on Friday and won't even tell me where he's at."

"How do you think I can help you?" I asked.

"Hell, I don't know. I can't go to the police on something like this, they're going to think Trey had something to do with Benny getting shot. I was thinking maybe you could find out who these people coming around are and maybe talk to them or scare them off or something."

"Look, Mr. Jenkins, I'll be honest

with you. I think the best course of action would be for Trey to come back to town and talk to the police about this, especially if he thinks the drug deal you're talking about might be related to Benny's murder."

"That's not going to happen. He knows he's in deep shit for getting involved in moving drugs in the first place but he sure as hell isn't going to voluntarily put himself in the middle of a murder investigation, and I can't say I blame him for that. There's always stories in the news about people getting sent away for murders they didn't do, and I see no reason to take that kind of risk right now. I've dealt with risk and reward my whole life and built a damn good business by trusting my instincts when it came to evaluating a risk. But with this situation there's no reward in the equation, only risk. And my son's freedom isn't something I want to him risk."

"I understand your point," I said. "Can you at least get Trey to talk to me? The only way I can help is if I know more about what's going on. And, you know as well as I do that Trey might not have been completely straight with you. It's pretty hard to be open and honest when you're talking to your father about something you've done that might disappoint the old man."

"Well, I can tell you right now he's not coming back to town for a while."

"Then find out where he is and I'll go talk to him there," I said. "It probably wouldn't be a good idea for you to go with me, since whoever is looking for him may be watching you. You don't want to lead them to him."

"Okay. I'll talk to him and see if I can get him to agree to that."

CHAPTER TWENTY-NINE
another three amigos

Ruidoso is located about five hours northwest of Elmore in the Sierra Blanca mountain range of New Mexico. It's a resort town catering to people wanting to escape the heat in the summer and find some snowy slopes to ski on in the winter, and a big percentage of its visitors come from Texas, the state next door to New Mexico.

When the oilfield activity in the Permian Basin region of eastern New Mexico and west Texas is booming, Ruidoso property values go up as those with extra cash from their oilfield businesses seek to invest in a family getaway spot not too far from home; at least not too far for people who routinely drive hundreds of miles in a week going between widely-scattered drilling locations. Of course, when boom turns to bust as it always does in the oil patch, the property values around Ruidoso inevitably fall as those same oilfield-dependent owners are forced to tighten their belts.

As I drove through downtown Ruidoso on my way to meet Trey Jenkins, the good health of the Permian Basin oilfield was pretty apparent. There were only a few vacant buildings and the restaurant parking lots were mostly full. Of course, it was still the off-season, with winter skiing at nearby Ski

Apache wrapped up and the real summer vacation traffic still a month away.

When I got to the west end of downtown I turned north on Mechem Drive and followed it as it wound through the mountains and led to the community of Alto, a planned residential development situated on a golf course. Dallas Jenkins had bought a house on the Alto golf course during one of the dips in the local real estate market, even though he admitted he hadn't set foot in it for several years. Trey used the house now and then for ski trips, but even Trey hadn't found time to visit lately. Until he needed a hideout.

The house looked deserted. There were no cars in sight and the shutters on the windows were closed. I parked in the driveway and a man wearing a golf shirt and jeans opened the front door and watched as I climbed out.

"Trey?" I asked.

"Yes sir. And, you must be Buddy."

He didn't look much like Dallas Jenkins and seemed to have a permanent pouting expression on his face.

We went inside, where a large TV was showing a golf tournament. He got two beers from the refrigerator and we sat down at a big granite-topped bar.

"Okay," he sighed after taking a long pull on his beer. "Where do I start."

"First of all," I said. "Your father wants me to help, but he understands that I'm not going to tell him everything I learn from you. You need to be completely straight with me, so I know exactly what we're dealing with."

"No problem," he said. "After all the shit that's gone down with Benny and all, I'm just looking for some help, and I don't mind telling you what an idiot I've been if it means getting this all straightened out."

He began by describing how he'd met a man named Sammy Rosado while on a fishing trip to Del Rio, Texas.

"My buddies and I used to go down there a lot, during college. There was this little bar we'd always end up going to at night because it was one of the few places we seemed to be able to hook up with girls. Anyway, I got to know Sammy Rosado there. It was actually Sammy's bar, as it turns out. He has some other people running it for him, but he owns it. So, we're talking about where I'm from and all that, and he mentions that he knows Benny Shanks, and I was like 'wow, it's a small world' cause I've known Benny like all my life."

"Turns out Benny is down there in Del Rio at the same time I am, and so the very next night we run into each other at Sammy's bar. We get to talking and then Sammy comes in and we end up all getting shit-faced together and talking about stuff until way after they close the doors. And sometime during the course of the night Benny starts talking about methamphetamine and how much of it is starting to flood into the States from Mexico. Of course, Benny's saying what an evil drug it is and everything, but I can see the dollar signs in his eyes when he talks about how it's rolling right down Main Street, through the middle of Elmore on its way to all those meth-heads up north in the bigger cities."

"See, I knew when I was back in high school that Benny was the source of the pot I was buying off another kid my age. So, I knew Benny wasn't any kind of virgin when it came to dealing drugs, and the way he kept talking about it, I could tell that he was sort of..."

"Laying out a business plan?" I offered.

"Yeah, exactly. He was laying out a business plan to see if he could get me and Sammy interested, or at least see if we had that kind of mindset. Kind of like when you're partying with people you don't really know and start dropping hints about smoking a joint to see if they pick up on it."

"Show me yours and I'll show you mine," I said.

"Yeah, that type of deal. Anyway,

so we get back together again the next night and keep kicking this subject of meth trafficking around, each of the three of us bringing it up at different times to show we might be willing to go along with the others if we got something going."

"What type of something?"

"Well, Benny really did think that meth was evil, but not so evil that he was completely opposed to making a buck off of it somehow. He just didn't want to be responsible for bringing meth to Elmore that would end up being sold on the streets there. His idea was to limit our involvement strictly to transportation, and only for stuff that was destined for other places. We'd be middle-men in the supply route and add on a reasonable markup for the risk we were taking."

"Sounds like Benny made a convincing argument."

"He did. Looking back on it now, it seems crazy to get involved in something like moving drugs, but Benny had a way of making it sound like just another business opportunity. Anyway, it turns out Sammy Rosado had a lot of connections in Mexico and knew exactly who to talk to on the other side of the border when it came to finding a source for meth. And, Benny knew somebody in Amarillo who had a connection that would buy as much as we could deliver to them on a regular basis."

"Unless I'm missing something," I said. "It almost sounds like Benny and Sammy had what they needed to start operating without you. But it also seems like the whole discussion and business proposition might have been planned in advance by Benny and Sammy. Did you ever think they might have been working together before you came into the picture?"

"I've thought about that a lot, especially over the last few days. I couldn't see it back then, but that would make a lot of sense now that I look back at it."

"So, what did you bring to the table that they needed to make their plan work."

"I guess it was the fact that we had a good reputation as being a legitimate business that used a lot of different kinds of trucks," he said. "There was this big construction project going on just outside Juarez, on the Mexican side of the border, and they were hiring subcontractors from the U.S. to work on it. Sammy knew somebody who could arrange for a truck that looked like it was going back and forth to work on that project to get through the Juarez border crossing checkpoint with no problem. Sammy had the idea of building two welding trucks that looked exactly the same, with a secret compartment that could be used to transport a load of meth when the trucks were coming north through the checkpoint and to transport cash when it was going south."

"Who built the trucks?"

"Sammy took care of that. They were pretty slick. The whole back end of the welding bed could be raised up and there was room to hide just about anything you needed to. I think they built them in Mexico. Those people down there are used to building all kinds of secret compartments in cars and shit."

"What happened after Sammy

had the trucks built?"

"We started making our runs. Small at first, until the people at both ends of the chain figured out they could trust us, and then we gradually started carrying more dope north and more cash south. Benny owned an old body shop building in Andrews, so the people from Amarillo would load up one of the welding trucks with cash to pay for the meth, weld the bed shut, drive it down and park it in the body shop in Andrews. Our driver would pick it up there and drive it down to Van Horn to an old pipe yard my dad owns. A driver from Juarez would be waiting there with the other truck, loaded with dope and with the bed welded shut. Our driver would switch trucks with the Juarez driver, drive the truck with the meth back to Andrews and park it in the body shop. A guy from Amarillo would pick it up and take it from there."

"You never touched the dope or the money?"

"Never."

"And when you say *our driver*, you mean Justin Ramey, don't you?"

"Yeah, that's right. Justin was making the runs. Benny set that up. Said he had somebody who could be our driver if I'd give him a job at Jenkins Drilling. Justin didn't really know what was going on. He just knew where to go and what to do and that it would mean an extra three hundred bucks in cash each time he made a run instead of spending his shift on a drilling rig somewhere."

"How did that work? Getting Justin away from his regular job to make the runs without anybody asking questions?"

"I just told his crew boss that I was setting up a side business for myself but wasn't ready to hire anybody full-time yet. Told him I needed Justin now and then for a few hours and then paid the crew boss an extra hundred each time to keep that information to himself."

"So, Justin Ramey was making a run the night he disappeared," I said.

"Yeah, he was. He was supposed to be back in town by midnight. He usually called when he was rolling through town towards Andrews and I'd leave a few minutes later, headed that direction too. Then, I'd pick him up at the body shop and drive him back here. But that night, he never called."

"What did you do?"

"I called Benny and told him Justin hadn't shown up on time.

He said to relax, that he'd probably had a flat or mechanical trouble with one of the trucks. So, I drove the route Justin was supposed to follow all the way to Van Horn. And then I got to the lot where they made the truck exchange and the gate was open. It's a fenced pipe yard and the gate is supposed to be closed and locked except when they're switching trucks, but it was standing wide open. So, I drove back to Elmore and waited until daylight to see if Justin called or showed up."

"And, this would be Wednesday morning, and Benny was shot the next Saturday, right?"

"Yeah, that's right. I talked to Benny again early Wednesday and we both went out looking. He drove north to Andrews in case something happened that direction and I went south to Van Horn again, driving a little slower and looking around in case Justin had to pull off the road far enough that I would have missed him in the dark."

"But, you didn't find anything," I said.

"No, and then Wednesday afternoon all hell starts to break loose. Benny calls his connection in Amarillo because he knows they've got a guy on his way down to pick up a truck full of dope they think is waiting. And, at the same time, Sammy Rosado starts calling and telling me that the truck with the money, the one Justin drove down to Van Horn, never showed up at the border crossing in Juarez and their driver hadn't been heard from."

"So, the truck with the dope and the truck with the money are both missing," I said.

"Right, and of course everybody wants answers from us and we don't know what the hell to tell them."

"How much dope and money are we talking about?" I asked

He shrugged. "I don't know how much dope, but this guy that Amarillo sent down has come to the office a couple of times telling me I need to come up with eight hundred grand."

"Do you think Justin knew why you had him making these runs?"

"No. He was curious, so I told him we were leasing the welding truck to a company from El Paso and we had an agreement with them to service the trucks every so often, that we rotated them out and left the one they weren't using with a guy in Andrews who worked on it, changed out the gas bottles on the back and that sort of thing."

"Think he bought that?"

"Oh, yeah. Justin ain't the brightest bulb in the chandelier."

Trey's cell phone rang.

"Hello."

He listened a few seconds and then leaned forward and put his beer down and looked visibly shaken.

"You're shitting me. Could they tell how it started?"

He stood up and began pacing back and forth as he listened to the party on the other end of the line.

"Oh, shit," he said suddenly. "What about Duke? Is he okay?"

He turned away from me as he listened, but I could tell from the way his shoulders slumped and he lowered his head that he didn't get the answer he was hoping for.

"No, that's okay," he said quietly. "Yeah, he showed up a few minutes ago. We're going over things right now."

After he finished his phone conversation, Trey excused himself and walked off down a hallway, giving me a chance to look around the cabin some more. There was a huge deer head mounted on a wall opposite the fire place and several other smaller sets of antlers along with half a dozen stuffed and mounted fish. The mantle was crowded with photographs of Dallas and Trey Jenkins and other people I didn't recognize on various outings, from what looked like an African safari to snow skiing trips to summertime lake outings. I recognized the Kona, Hawaii fishing docks in one photo of a much younger Dallas Jenkins standing beside a huge tuna suspended in the air.

When Trey returned he grabbed another beer from the refrigerator before taking his seat again.

"That was my dad that called. The sons of bitches burned my house down," he said. "My dog was inside. I knew I shouldn't have left him there by himself."

"Do they think it was arson?"

"Yeah. Dad said it went up really quick, and it looked like they broke in first and the fire department found two empty gas cans inside the house. I know they must have shot Duke when they went inside. He never would have let them come in there like that."

"How much do you know about the people you were dealing with on the drug runs?" I asked.

"Not much. I've already told you about Sammy Rosado. He's the only name I know on that end of the deal. As far as the people in Amarillo go, Benny took care of all that, and he never used any names when we talked about it. He'd always say *the guy in Amarillo* or *the people up north*. To tell you the truth, I didn't really *want* to know any names. I was happy to let Sammy and Benny handle it all, since I thought that kept me a little bit insulated and safe. I guess I was wrong about that though, wasn't I?"

"Do think there's a chance Justin knew why he was making the truck runs and might have been involved in planning the hijacking?" I asked.

"No way. Like I said Justin was clueless as to what was going on, and I don't think he's smart enough or has enough balls to do something like that. Besides, I brought up that possibility to Benny at first and he seemed to consider it, but then a couple of days later he brought it up again and emphasized that he knew for sure that Justin wasn't involved. Like he knew more about the situation at that point."

"What do you think he may have learned?" I asked.

"I don't know. Benny didn't share a lot of information if he didn't have to. But, everybody was sure pointing fingers at Justin. Maybe Benny was just trying to protect him until he could find out what was going on."

CHAPTER THIRTY
ribeye

I left Trey Jenkins at his family's cabin in Alto and drove back to Ruidoso, where I had a steak dinner alone at a local restaurant and then spent the night in a motel in the middle of town. Trey had offered to let me spend the night in one of the guest rooms at the Jenkins cabin, but I needed some time to myself to think about what my next move should be and to re-evaluate my uncomfortable position of having one foot inside the Elmore Police Department and the other in the middle of a group of some feuding drug traffickers.

I couldn't bring myself to muster up much sympathy for Trey Jenkins and the predicament he found himself in, and it would be easy to say that karma just finally caught up with Benny Shanks, but to me it looked like Justin Ramey was a true victim of circumstances here. And, right now working with the information Trey Jenkins provided was my only hope of finding out what happened to Justin and getting him back home, if he was even still alive.

I also had to think about Norris Jackson and how his gambling debt to Benny would keep him on the Elmore PD's short list of murder suspects until I could find enough information for Clemmer to cross him off. I hadn't given a lot of thought to the possibility that Norris might actually have something to do with the shooting, but in the back of my mind I knew it was a mistake to rule anybody out with so little information to go on.

On the surface, it was starting to look like Benny Shanks had died at the hands of someone working for Sammy Rosado's Juarez connection or Benny's contacts in Amarillo, both parties having equally compelling of motives for the murder. But, I also knew I couldn't rule out Trey Jenkins or Sammy Rosado, since the disappearance of the dope and money had instantly driven a wedge of distrust between each man and his other partners. Eight hundred thousand dollars in cash and a load of methamphetamine worth an equal amount in wholesale value provided plenty of reasons for each of the partners to question what happened and who might have been involved.

CHAPTER THIRTY-ONE
home again

I got an early start back to Elmore the next morning and was almost to the New Mexico-Texas state line when I got a call from Sandy Doyle, a contact from Odessa who tended to spend more time on the wrong side of the law than the right side.

Although the call came from out of the blue, I was glad to hear from Sandy. I knew that if I was going to dig any deeper into Justin Ramey's disappearance and Benny

Shanks' murder, I would need a lot more information about the people involved. And, if there was anybody in west Texas who knew about the players in the illegal drug business in the region it was Sandy Doyle, who was the closest thing to an old-school organized crime figure I had ever known; a true throwback to an earlier era.

When I first came back to Elmore after retiring from the homicide division of the Austin Police Department, I had a brush with Sandy Doyle while investigating another case. While my actions to resolve the situation had put the two of us at odds, when all was said and done, we ended up with an uneasy stalemate that kept us on speaking terms.

One thing you learn as a career police officer is that people who are engaged in criminal activity as a way of life don't respond well to anyone from law enforcement that openly disrespects them. That's why the most successful street cops are those that can look beyond even the most offensive actions and see the problems, needs and motivations of the human being behind them. Those same skills are what allow homicide investigators to connect with accused murderers, gain their trust, and eventually lead them to making a confession. So, while I might not approve of the things that Sandy Doyle did, I understood the value of being able to talk to him one on one about what kind of operation Benny Shanks and Sammy Rosado might have set up.

But, I also needed to talk to Sandy Doyle for another reason. To explore the possibility that he was the one responsible for

Benny's murder. According to Norris Jackson, local law enforcement had always felt pretty confident in the knowledge that Benny Shanks' drug activity was limited to marijuana, whereas Sandy Doyle and his associates were responsible for the movement of harder drugs like heroin, crack cocaine and methamphetamine. I couldn't believe that Benny Shanks had become involved in an operation to move large amounts of meth through the area without paying Sandy Doyle a percentage of the profits, or without at least getting his approval. More than one of Sandy's associates had made similar mistakes over the years and many of them had paid for it with their lives. Benny had always seemed too smart to try to beat the odds when dealing with Sandy.

"Where you at?" Sandy barked.

I told him I was out sightseeing.

"You need to come see me, and the sooner the better," he said, hanging up before I could respond..

CHAPTER THIRTY-TWO
crying time again

When I got back to Elmore, I stopped by the house to check on things and see if the small herd of feral cats that I looked after needed more food or water. Then, I drove thirty minutes south to Odessa and found the strip mall where Doyle Finance, the front for Sandy Doyle's operation, was located.

The young women manning the desks at the front of the building were all busy, either interviewing potential loan candidates, texting their friends or checking their Facebook pages, so I walked on down the hallway that I knew led to Sandy Doyle's office.

He sat behind his desk, leaning forward and speaking quietly to a young Hispanic woman who looked to be in her mid-twenties. I stood in the doorway for a few seconds before he glanced up and saw me.

"Try not to worry about it, okay?" he said to the young woman. "We'll talk about it some more tomorrow, but right now this man here needs to see me."

He stood up and watched her go and then gestured for me to sit down.

"These kids I got working for me," he said, shaking his head. "This one's got a husband that's been in prison for a year and she just figured out she's three months pregnant. So, she comes to me with it. Like I can do something about it."

"I don't know Sandy, I hear you're a pretty powerful guy," I said.

He laughed.

"Politicians and horse races, I got a pretty good handle on. Mother Nature? I got no juice there. Know what I mean? Now, what the hell can I do for you?"

"You called this meeting," I said. "Anything you'd like to confess?"

"You sound just like my damn priest, except he's always trying to get me to write a check to go along with the confession. I tell you, when I pass on there better damn well be a chapel or something built around here with my name on it, as many checks as I've written those sorry money-changers."

"St. Sandy's Catholic School," I

said. "It does have a nice ring to it."

"Don't it? But no, I don't have anything I wanna confess."

"I didn't think you would. But, when you called I was hoping you might help me get an understanding of what went on with our mutual acquaintance, and what kind of business deal he may have been involved in."

"Now you're talking like a damn cop again. What'd you do, re-enlist or something? Sign up for another tour of duty?"

"No, I'm still on my own," I said. "Just a guy with a curious mind."

"Well then stop talkin' like you're wearing a wire or something. We had one dance together already, so you don't have to tiptoe around it; *mutual acquaintance* this and *business deal* that."

"Okay," I said. "Benny Shanks.

You got anything for me?"

He thought about his answer for a few seconds.

"First of all," he said. "What do you think you know about Benny and this business deal you mentioned?"

"I think he was involved in moving some meth through this area," I said. "And, back when I was still a cop we had these training sessions and they always taught us that in the illegal drug business the concept of territory was real important. They said that if Party A controlled the territory that Party B wanted to move drugs through, that Party B better be prepared to give Party A a piece of the pie or the party might be all over for Party B before it even got started."

He nodded. "Sounds logical."

"And," I continued. "Back when I

was attending Elmore High School a couple dozen years ago, we all knew that Benny Shanks was the main source of pot in town, even if he used somebody else to sell it. But, what happened since then? Did he diversify into selling crystal meth to school kids?"

Sandy shook his head.

"Listen," he said. "I don't know if you came here expecting me to whadda ya call it, speak ill of the dead, but if you did, I got nothing to say."

"Then why did you call? I'm just trying to understand if Benny ventured into an area of business where he was infringing on someone else's territory. That's all."

He shrugged. "I called about something else entirely. But, how would I know what Benny was up to? Sure, he was a friend, but I never knew every move he made. He was his own guy."

"He didn't work for you?"

"No, never. Now, I'm sure you understand that we may have had a business partnership or two over the years, and we helped each other out when the opportunity came up. But, did I tell Benny what to do? No, I did not."

"Do you know someone named Sammy Rosado?" I asked.

He looked at me for a couple of seconds before answering.

"I've heard the name. 'Course there could be a lot of guys around with that name."

"What about some outfit from Amarillo that Benny may have been doing some business with?"

He smiled.

"Amarillo? Oh, yeah that's the big town up north of Lubbock where they have that famous steakhouse.

I've heard of that too. Boy, you really don't have much to go on, do you?"

"That's why I'm here at the seat of knowledge," I said. "When you called I was hoping you could help fill in the blanks."

"Jeez, first the pregnant secretary and now you. I feel like the only grown-up on the planet. Okay, I'm gonna go through it with you, but everything I say is just all hypothetical and between the two of us."

"Understood," I said.

"It sounds like you've probably figured most of it out," he said. "Benny and Sammy Rosado had a deal to move some meth through the area on a regular basis, from just inside the border to a guy from Amarillo named Frank Delano, who has connections to somebody in the Northeast somewhere."

"Sammy Rosado had a connection in Mexico?" I said, repeating what Trey Jenkins had told me.

Sandy shrugged. "Maybe. Maybe not. It's hard to say who you're really dealing with when that stuff comes out of Mexico. The cartels are always fighting to take over each other's territory, and you've got other guys who are just loosely connected to the cartels, and then some guys who just do their own thing until somebody from the cartels catches them and puts them out of business. Permanently."

"Do you think Benny's shooting could have been a cartel thing?"

"That's always a possibility," he said. "But, remember what they taught you in cop school, territory is pretty important in the drug trade. Party A and Party B and all that stuff."

"Well, if Benny and Sammy were Party B, then who would be Party A that controlled the territory they were moving meth through?"

"Hypothetically speaking again, of course," he continued. "There is a guy from down in Houston named Reggie Marshall. Ever heard of him?"

I shook my head.

"Well, I'm not real surprised," he said. "Reggie keeps a pretty low profile and stays pretty well insulated. But, he's very territorial, and over the past few years has developed the attitude that if anything fucking moves out here, he has the right to tax it."

"It sounds like you don't necessarily agree," I said.

"What are you gonna do?" he said. "Sometimes you have to pick your battles. That's what I tried to tell my friend Benny. Reggie

Marshall decided he wanted a piece of Benny's action, and Benny wasn't willing to give it up. Reggie came to me and wanted me to talk to Benny, so I did. I told Benny it wasn't worth going up against Reggie. But, there was something about the way Reggie approached Benny that just stuck in Benny's craw. And, that Benny could be one stubborn son of a bitch once he made his mind up about something."

"How did Reggie react when he found out Benny wasn't going to play ball?"

"Oh, I'm sure he was pissed. And, I know your next question. Was he pissed enough to kill Benny? I doubt it. One thing about Reggie is he's practical and he's a businessman. And, he knows there's always more than one way to get what he wants."

"What do you mean?" I asked.

"Reggie might have decided that if Benny wasn't going to share, then he'd just throw a monkey wrench into the whole setup."

"By hijacking both sides of a drug deal at the same time?" I asked.

He smiled. "I'm not saying I know that's what happened, but wouldn't that be the perfect way for him to get Benny right where he wanted him? Say Reggie's guys grab both the money and the dope. Benny's stuck in the middle of a deal that's gone south and Reggie's sitting there with everything needed to put it together again. Except now he's in the perfect position to negotiate an even better royalty from Benny than he was originally asking for."

"In that situation it wouldn't make much sense for Reggie Marshall to kill Benny," I said. "Benny had the apparatus in place to start the shipments up again, which would generate a new income stream for Marshall."

"That's right," he said. "But, this is all just speculation. I don't know if Reggie Marshall's guys were really behind that hijacking or not. I only know that Benny called me the next day and that's what he thought. And, he was more worried about what happened to his nephew than the dope or the money. I mean over a million and a half in product and cash missing and he just wants to find out what happened to this goofy kid. That's the kind of guy Benny was though."

He stopped talking and looked away for a second as his eyes got moist.

"Christ, look at me," he said, shaking his head. "I'm about to start blubbering like a little girl."

He pointed a finger at me.

"You tell anybody you saw Sandy Doyle crying and I'll cut your balls off, you hear?"

"Your secret's safe with me," I said. "But, I've got to ask myself, why would you give me your theory about how things went down? You're not the kind of guy that goes out of his way to help law enforcement, so why would you help me?"

"Well I sure as hell ain't ratting on anybody. I just told you my theory, and Benny's theory. Now if this theory turns out to be right and telling you about it causes Reggie Marshall some trouble, well I won't lose any sleep over it."

"Life would be easier without Reggie Marshall looking over your shoulder?" I asked.

"Something like that."

"What do you think happened to Benny's nephew?" I asked.

"Well, the fact that he hasn't turned up yet ain't a good sign," he said. "Things could've gotten out of hand. It happens."

There was a knock on the door frame as one of the women from the desks out front brought Sandy a check to sign. When he finished signing he asked her to close the door on her way out.

"Okay, now for the real reason I called you," he said, after she'd gone. "There's something else we need to talk about. It has to do with how we left things with that other situation a while back. With that Sheriff friend of yours."

He was referring to the earlier case that I had resolved by asking Norris Jackson to hold onto a crucial piece of evidence as insurance to protect those involved in the case and make sure Sandy and everyone else involved held up their end of the deal.

"It's really kind of funny how things work out," he said. "Like I mentioned earlier, Benny and I were involved in some business deals over the years, and we got to be pretty close. We used to spend time together with our wives back when we were younger. Do you know Benny's wife, Maria?"

"I do. Nice lady."

"Oh, yeah. And, pretty smart too. She kept things afloat for some long stretches over the years when Benny had to spend time in Huntsville. Really has a head for business. Anyway, Benny and I had an agreement that if he passed on while we were both still in business, that I would try to help Maria out where I could. Maybe help her liquidate some of Benny's assets."

"What are you getting at? What kind of assets?"

He waved a hand around. "Did you happen to notice the sign outside when you came in? Doyle Finance? Our friend Benny was in the finance business too, you know. He was holding paper on a lot of people around your little town when he passed. So, I did what I could to help Maria out by giving her a way to liquidate all that paper."

"Well, that was nice of you," I said, knowing what must surely be coming next.

"Lots of interesting names in Benny's books," he said. "People in all walks of life it seems."

He rummaged under a pile of papers and brought out a dog-eared green ledger book.

"Now, I usually keep this sort of

thing confidential," he said. "But, I feel like we've got a kind of understanding, and I just thought you might find some of these names interesting."

He rattled off a list of half a dozen names and I recognized a few from seeing their names attached to local businesses or reading about them in the newspaper doing something charitable for the community.

"And wait, one of the biggest amounts on here was from a doctor I think. Let's see... oh, yeah, Dr. Tyler Drake. Those doctors always have expensive tastes, don't they? Oh, and look here, underneath the doctor, here's another guy who owes a bundle. Well, would you look at that? It's our mutual friend, Sheriff Norris Jackson."

I didn't respond but felt a pang of

guilt that I hadn't allowed myself to think through what might happen to Norris' debt to Benny now that Benny was dead. Maria selling Benny's gambling accounts to Sandy Doyle made perfect sense of course but gave Sandy some new leverage in that old situation that involved Norris, Sandy and me. Now that Sandy held Norris' gambling debt I knew he wouldn't be able to resist the temptation to try to use it as a bargaining tool to change the terms of the deal we'd negotiated earlier.

"Give me a figure," I said.

"Whadda ya mean?"

"I mean figure up how much Norris needs to pay to square his account with you today, and a daily figure for the vig. Norris was getting ready to pay up when Benny got shot," I lied. "Give me a figure and I'll get you the money."

He gave me a funny look.

"Well that's a hell of a note. I got a book full of new customers here and you come in here and tell me I don't get the chance to develop a relationship with one of them? And, from the number of the entries in the book, it looks like Sheriff Jackson could be a real good customer."

I shrugged. "You're not going to cry again are you?"

CHAPTER THIRTY-THREE
background check

Visiting Sandy Doyle had paid off. I now had a clearer picture of how the drug transport arrangement worked, and the name of another player in the operation; Frank Delano. I also had Reggie Marshall to throw into the mix as the possible force behind the hijacking of the welding truck. Driving back from Odessa, I thought about Sandy using Benny Shanks' gambling book as a way to set up shop in Elmore with a list of already established customers. Sandy Doyle hadn't built his illicit empire by missing opportunities when they were presented, and while his momentary tears over the death of Benny Shanks may have been genuine, he wasn't going to let his grief keep him from moving in to take over what had been Benny's territory. I knew I'd be running into Sandy Doyle and his men a lot closer to home in the future. That was one reason I wanted to try to get Norris Jackson's debt with Sandy cleared up. I didn't trust Sandy Doyle to be as accommodating and discreet about Norris' gambling debts as Benny Shanks had been. My plan was to use some of my savings to pay Doyle off and get Norris off the hook. I just didn't know how I'd explain what I was going to do to Norris without making him angry, ashamed or both.

It wasn't until I was back in Elmore and close to my office that I remembered another name Sandy Doyle had mentioned when talking about Benny's gambling book. Dr. Tyler Drake was the doctor who had given me my physical exam a few days earlier, in a medical clinic that Benny Shanks had owned. I'd known plenty of doctors with gambling and/or financial problems, so it wasn't surprising that a doctor's name might turn up on Benny's books, but the fact that Drake actually worked for Benny was interesting. I decided it might be a good idea to find out more about him and look into whether he might have anything to gain from Benny's death, aside from the possible erasure of a personal debt.

A few minutes spent searching the internet revealed that Dr. Tyler Drake had been a partner in a small medical practice located in a suburb of Dallas prior to moving to Elmore. The website associated with the practice listed Dr. Michael Boxer as the administrator, so decided to give him a call. I told the young woman who answered that I was calling from a private hospital outside Austin and wanted to discuss Tyler Drake with Dr. Boxer.

"He doesn't work here anymore," she said, trying to see if that would be enough information to send me on my way.

"Dr. Boxer doesn't work there anymore?" I asked, just trying to be difficult.

"No, Dr. Tyler Drake doesn't work here anymore. He left here quite a while ago."

"Ah, okay. Well, I was really just calling to get some informal feedback about how Dr. Drake was to work with. Nothing official, you understand. I was hoping to talk to Dr. Boxer to get his opinion."

"Dr. Boxer is in Costa Rica until next week, and he may not want to talk about Dr. Drake anyway, for legal reasons."

"Oh, really? Did you work there before Dr. Drake left?" I asked.

"Yes, I did. Unfortunately."

"This isn't sounding good," I said, laughing. "It doesn't sound like you miss him very much."

"Believe me, I don't."

"That bad, huh? Anything you can talk about? And, again this is strictly off the record. We just received his resume in the mail and haven't even contacted him for an interview yet. I'm just asking so I'll know what kind of problems

I'll be avoiding by sticking this in a filing cabinet and forgetting about it."

"Well, if this is off the record I don't guess it could hurt. Lots of people around here know what happened. It isn't any secret that he had money problems and left here owing the other doctors a bundle."

"This sounds like a story I've heard before," I said. "These doctors think they've got to put up a certain appearance to others and they just live way beyond their means. I'll bet Dr. Drake drove an expensive car and lived in a mansion."

"Well, he did have a pretty nice car," she said. "Some kind of Chrysler, I think. But, he lived in an apartment complex instead of a mansion. No, his problem wasn't the money he spent, it was the money he gambled on football and basketball."

"Lots of trips out to Las Vegas?" I asked.

"Oh, no. He had a bookie that used to call all the time and leave messages for Dr. Drake to call him. I mean, we've all got personal lives, but they didn't hire me to be spending my day taking all these personal messages for Dr. Drake and trying to explain to his bookie why the doctor wouldn't call him back. It got to be a constant problem. And, Dr. Drake wasn't too interested in practicing medicine either. He'd have a patient waiting in an exam room for an hour while he'd be in his office watching a game on TV or checking scores on his computer."

"And the rest of you had to cover for him," I said. "So, what finally happened?"

"Well, the rest of the doctors were just about ready to send him packing when he up and quit one day. I heard he moved to some little town down around the Midland-Odessa area."

"Just like that, huh?"

"Just like that," she said. "And, not a moment too soon, in my opinion."

CHAPTER THIRTY-FOUR
drop cloth

"I really think the color will grow on you," Angie was saying as she swept in carrying a big plastic bag emblazoned with the Dairy Queen logo.

We had spent the morning repainting the kitchen in my parents' house before she ran to town to pick up our lunch. I washed the worst of the paint off my hands while she set up an impromptu picnic on the back porch.

I had been giving her a rundown on the latest developments all morning while we painted.

"I guess that explains all those rumors about Dallas Jenkins," she had said after I related Trey Jenkins' confession. "I never even considered the possibility that Trey might be mixed up in something like that."

"Just talking to Dallas when he came to me for help it was pretty clear that he never knew what was going on, and Trey just got in over his head. Of course, a lot of guys sitting in prison just got in over their heads too."

"I don't think I can look at Trey the same way again," she said. "How do you do it? How do you look at somebody like Benny, who was moving huge amounts of drugs that are ruining so many peoples' lives, and care enough about him to want to solve his murder?"

I thought about that one a second.

"I guess I learned a long time ago to look to try to find the innocent part inside everybody, no matter how bad they appear to be on the outside. We all start out as truly innocent when we're babies, and then we each get corrupted to a certain degree the older we get. Some, like Benny, more than others. I try to imagine the six-year-old Benny that lived inside the old man with a rap sheet a mile long. That kid didn't deserve to be killed, just like any human being, no matter how evil, doesn't deserve it."

"But how do you square that with your stand on capital punishment?" she said.

"You were asking me about the

attitude I put on when I go out to solve a murder. It gets a little more complicated once the murder is solved and you start considering the question of justice."

We ate in silence for a while, closely observed by a growing audience of patiently waiting cats hoping to be rewarded with a meal of our leftovers.

"What's your next move?" she asked a few minutes later.

"Well, Sandy Doyle gave me some more people to check out, and knowing Trey Jenkins' side of the story will help."

"So, you do what? Start poking around in more people's business?"

"That's really the only way to get results. Poking around in other people's business."

CHAPTER THIRTY-FIVE
coffee date

I called Madison Miller at Wildcatter Chevrolet and asked if I could meet her at the Yucca Inn for a cup of coffee.

"Another coffee date?" she said as she sat down across from me. "Mister, I told you the way to my heart is a big steak dinner with all the trimmings."

We talked about the car dealership for a few minutes before I steered the conversation toward the local economy and from there to how difficult it was for some of the local oilfield businesses to find qualified workers.

"It's all changed so much from when I was a kid," I said. "Now they've got to screen everybody for drugs and make sure everybody's passed a physical exam. I had to go get a drug test done a few weeks ago and I went to that Petro-Tex Medical place to get it done. That doctor who runs that has got to be making a killing doing all those tests."

"Oh, yeah," she said. "Dr. Drake. You know the only reason he came down here to Elmore was because Benny told him they needed to open up a medical place like that."

"Really? That's interesting. How did they know each other?"

"Benny and I met him a few years ago, at a Cowboys game. We had gone to Dallas for the game and were watching it from one of those VIP boxes at the new stadium right after it opened. I can't remember whose box it was. Probably somebody that used Benny to handle their bets. Anyway, Dr. Drake was there with his girlfriend and we all kind of hung out together for most of the game."

"So, how long after that was it that Dr. Drake opened Petro-Tex Medical?"

"Oh, it was a few months, maybe close to a year before he and his girlfriend moved down here. Benny helped him find a building and set him up with some people who fixed it up and got it ready. Either Benny bought the building, or went in partners with Dr. Drake, or something like that. Like I told you before, Benny never really let me in on the details of a lot of his business dealings."

"Did you and Benny ever get together with Dr. Drake after he moved down here?"

"No, but Benny and I didn't do a whole lot in public around here anyway. And, I don't think Benny really cared much for Dr. Drake as a person. It seemed like they developed some friction between them once Dr. Drake moved down here. Benny said something one time about Dr. Drake thinking he was better than everybody else. Benny gave him a lot of help getting set up in business here, but then after that it seemed like Dr. Drake resented having Benny as a partner, like he didn't want Benny around."

"Sounds kind of ungrateful," I said.

"That's exactly what I thought," she said.

CHAPTER THIRTY-SIX
good test bad test

When I started looking into Dr. Tyler Drake and his medical practice, which included processing drug screening tests for job applicants, I remembered what Sheryl at Jenkins Drilling had told me about some of the people they had hired through Benny Shanks' company Field Hands. She had said that some of those job applicants had been hired with clean drug tests, but later failed random drug tests conducted by the company. That, coupled with the offer of "expedited service" from the receptionist at Field Hands that seemed to guarantee a clean drug test, made me suspect that Dr. Drake might be putting out false drug test results for any job applicants who went through Benny's company to get a job.

I decided to follow up on that and called Dallas Jenkins to ask about the possibility of talking to Sheryl again.

"Well hell, that's no problem," he said. "I'll tell her to be expecting you."

A few minutes later, I was sitting next to Sheryl in front of a file cabinet full of personnel files.

"Okay, here's another one that I remember," she said. "We drew his name for the piss-in-a-bottle lottery less than a week after he came to work here and he tested positive for meth and pot. He was another one from Field Hands."

She flipped through the file until she found a pink form with the Petro-Tex logo printed on it

"Here's the original drug screening form that we get from Petro-Tex."

The form was signed with a scribble that looked like it could be Tyler Drake's signature.

"You said you draw the names at random that you test?" I asked.

"Yes, we do now. When we first started using Petro-Tex, they would do the drawing and give us the names of who to test, but we started noticing that they never drew anybody we hired through Field Hands, so we thought maybe they didn't have everybody included in the pool of people they were drawing from. That's when we started doing the drawing ourselves."

"When somebody gets their name selected, how does the test work?" I asked.

"We give them a plastic container with a number on it and they pee in it and give it back. Then, we send it over to Petro-Tex and they send us back a report on whether it was positive for any drugs."

"Do you send the employee's name with the sample?"

"No, it's just that number, which we assign to the employee when we pick them for testing. We get a report back that has the number on it and then match it up to the employee in our system."

"But, I notice that this report here, for the employee you hired through Field Hands does have the employee's name on it."

"That's because you're looking at the original drug test was part of his pre-screening physical before we hired him. Here, let me see the file."

She flipped to another section of the file and found another drug test report, also from Petro-Tex. This one had a different signature

"See, this test, which is the one that came back positive and got the employee fired, only has the number we assigned when we did our random test, no name."

"I see. When you send the random testing samples over to Petro-Tex, they don't have any way of knowing who the sample came from. As opposed to how it works when somebody goes there for their initial physical and screening and their name is on the paperwork."

"That's correct," she said. "And, I've got a dozen more just like this one, guys we hired through Field

Hands who turned out to be dopers even though they came here with clean drug tests."

"Seems like more than a coincidence," I said.

"It does, don't it?"

CHAPTER THIRTY-SEVEN
pee cup two

When I stepped up to the sliding glass window in the Petro-Tex Medical reception area, Maxine recognized me immediately.

"I knew you'd be back," she said, handing me a clipboard with a form just like the one I'd filled out on my first visit. "You got a better job offer, didn't you?"

"Something like that," I said. "Do I get a discount for coming back in so soon?"

"Sorry, Charlie. We've got to run

all the same tests, so it costs just the same as the last time."

"I guess the people who do your lab work don't give y'all a discount just because one of us came back in again," I said.

"Oh, we do all of our lab work in-house."

"Really. Are y'all hiring now? I was pretty good in chemistry class back in high school."

"Honey, Dr. Drake does all of the lab work himself. That's why we charge a little more. You get an actual doctor doing all the behind the scenes work instead of just sending your sample off somewhere."

"Isn't that something?" I said. "I hadn't thought about it much, but I guess I like the idea that not just anybody can get ahold of a sample of my pee. He processes all those samples by himself?"

"He does now." She lowered her voice and glanced around. "He used to have an assistant. She was actually his girlfriend too, but they broke up. She doesn't work here anymore and Dr. Drake does it all by himself."

"Was she kind of a heavyset redhead gal?" I asked.

"Oh, no. She's a skinny little thing with bleached blonde hair."

"Huh. I thought I might have known her. Is her name Melanie? I think I met a Melanie one time that said she worked here before she went to work for that bank out on 385."

"No, it's Amber. Amber Branson. And, she moved to Midland after she broke up with the doctor. I heard she was working for an insurance agency there."

"Well, everybody's got to have insurance," I said.

"Death, taxes, insurance and drug tests," she said, smiling as she held out an empty urine sample cup.

CHAPTER THIRTY-EIGHT
doctor ex

It didn't take long to track down Amber Branson once Maxine remembered that she'd heard it was a State Farm agency where Amber had landed. I got lucky and hit the right agency on my third phone call and used my charm and creativity to convince Amber to meet me for a drink after work.

We met at a place called The Wine Rack, not far from where Amber worked. I misled her slightly on the phone by telling her

I worked for a group of investors that were looking for "quality people" for a startup company to be headquartered in Midland.

As we sat waiting for drinks and making small talk, I could tell she was intrigued by the idea of a potential job offer but reserved enough to not come right out and ask for more information. Once our drinks arrived and I felt like we had a good rapport going, I lowered the boom.

"Amber, I've got to confess something. I'm a private investigator, and I'm actually working for the Amalgamated Global Reinsurance Corporation. They're a big company that's behind a lot of the companies that provide malpractice insurance to thousands of doctors around the country, including Dr. Tyler Drake. I understand that you know Dr.

Drake."

Her expression went from one of pleasant interest to confusion and then to wariness.

"Yes, I know him," she offered.

"And, I know that you were in a relationship with Dr. Drake, and that you worked in his office for a time," I said.

"Okay. Yeah, that's right. But, we haven't been together for a while now. Quite a while."

"But, you knew how things operated around his practice?"

"Well, I did work there for a while, like you said. But, you know what?" she said, scooting back from the table and starting to pick up her purse. "I think it was pretty shitty of you to lie to me, just to get me to meet you here so you could start asking me about something completely different. I think I'm done here."

I reached up and gently put a hand on her forearm.

"You might want to hear about why I'm here before you go. I think it would be in your best interest."

She slowly put her purse on the table and sat back down.

I glanced around and lowered my voice. "The people that hired me are especially interested in how Dr. Drake handled the drug testing part of the business."

I could see her tense up even in the dim light of the lounge.

"I don't know anything about that," she said, flatly.

"Well, maybe you don't. But, I've already talked to three people who told me that you were directly involved with the drug testing."

She looked off toward the front door and chewed on her lower lip for a few seconds.

"Am I in some kind of trouble here? I mean, do I need to talk to a lawyer?"

"Right now, I'm just gathering information," I said. "And, like I told you, I'm a private investigator, and this is more about Dr. Drake's malpractice insurance than anything else. I'm just trying to figure out what goes on inside Dr. Drake's practice so I can report it back to the insurance company. My guess is that the worst that can happen would be Dr. Drake gets his insurance canceled and maybe they refer his conduct to some kind of medical board. I don't see how this could turn into anything that you need to worry about. Not from my end, anyway."

She relaxed a little and gave her head a quick shake, then downed the last of her drink and held up the empty glass.

"In that case, can I get me another one of these?"

The waitress delivered new drinks and I waited until she was out of earshot to speak.

"As I said, I'm just gathering information, and I most likely won't even mention your name in my report. But, the drug testing. Could you walk me through that a little bit? How it works?"

"Well, as I'm sure you know, drug testing is a big deal around the oilfield here. All these companies have millions of dollars invested in their equipment, and there are lives at stake anytime their employees are operating it. They want everybody to be safe. Plus, they can't get contracts to work with other companies unless they can satisfy OSHA and everybody else that their employees are clean. So, all these companies have got some kind of random drug testing program to make sure their workers aren't high when they're out there working. And, they all need somebody to process those drug tests and report on them. There is a high demand for what Petro-Tex Medical does. "

"Is that why Dr. Drake moved to Elmore? To take advantage of the demand for that kind of work?" I asked.

"Mmm. Sorta, but no, not really," she said. "See, long story short, Tyler owed somebody a bunch of money and was basically forced to move to Elmore to start the clinic as a way of paying him back."

"Benny Shanks?" I asked.

She looked startled at the mention of his name.

"Yes, Benny Shanks," she answered slowly. "Tyler had a gambling problem. At first, I thought Benny was just a guy that Tyler liked to hang out with, but it turns out Benny was like a loan shark or something. Tyler owed him a ton of money. I thought that Benny was going to have Tyler killed or something, but instead Benny made Tyler move to Elmore and then put up even more money to start Petro-Tex Medical."

"And you?"

"I moved to Elmore with him. Probably one of the stupidest things I've ever done. I should have split up with Tyler when I found out he owed Benny so much money, but I just let myself get deeper and deeper into it. I ended up doing some things I'm not proud of, but I guess like they say, hindsight is twenty-twenty."

"What do you regret the most?"

"Probably the drug tests," she said. "Like I mentioned, it's extremely dangerous out there in the oilfield, and I look back and think that I could have been responsible for putting somebody out there on a job that could have accidentally killed people."

"How did the drug tests work?"

"A lot of the tests we ran were processed normally, and I never knew there was anything funny going on. Then, I realized that any time there was a drug test done for Field Hands, which is Benny's company, that Tyler would insist he be the one to process the test. I thought it was kind of odd, so I started paying attention to what was going on and happened to see Tyler intentionally switch the results on some tests for Field Hands so that a test that came up dirty was reported as clean."

"Did you ask him about it?" I asked.

"I did. It took me a while to get the courage to ask, but when I did, Tyler told me the whole story. He said he owed Benny Shanks well over a million dollars counting the gambling debts and startup money for Petro-Tex. Part of his arrangement with Benny meant that Tyler had to make sure that anytime Field Hands wanted a certain drug test to come back clean that it would."

"Just like that."

"Just like that," she said. "Tyler said he even went to a bank about borrowing enough money to get settled up with Benny, but Benny's name was on all the assets and Benny blocked him from doing it. Benny needed Tyler right where he was so he could continue to get clean drug tests on his employees."

"So, what caused you to leave Petro-Tex?" I asked.

"It was a combination of things," she said. "I started to see Tyler for the person he really was. I mean when we started out together I thought he was wonderful. This young, handsome doctor with a nice house and car. I grew up in Littlefield and never dreamed I'd end up with a doctor, so I was a little bit starry-eyed in the beginning. But, once we moved to Elmore and I found out what was going on with the drug tests, and then ended up right in the middle of it by helping Tyler to falsify the results, well it was just a little too much. And, it got little bit scary for me."

"What do you mean?"

"One weekend, when the clinic was closed, we went in to do the lab work. We were always behind on it since Tyler couldn't trust anybody from the outside to process the results. Anyway, this guy somehow got into the building while we were there, thinking we had some kind of drugs on the premises or something. Tyler finally convinced him we didn't have any and got the guy to leave, but we were both pretty shook up. Tyler told Benny about it and Benny arranged to get Tyler a gun from a private dealer he knew. So, from then on, Tyler always carried that gun, and it never made me feel any safer. Just the opposite."

"Do you know what kind of gun it was? In case the people who hired me ask."

"No, I just know how it made Tyler act when he had it with him."

"How did he act?"

"Like he would jump at the chance to shoot somebody."

CHAPTER THIRTY-NINE
head south

The next morning another piece of the puzzle fell into place when Shane Gerber, the DEA agent from El Paso called with some news.

"We had an interesting call yesterday from an agent working down in Fort Hancock," he said. "There's a border crossing there and something turned up on the other side. Seems the Mexican Army came across an abandoned welding truck outside of El Porvenir and there was a decapitated corpse inside. Then they noticed the guy's head stuck on a fencepost nearby. We thought it might be related to that truck you found up your way since it had the same kind of hidden compartment that Sheriff Crabtree described."

"Probably is," I said. "I've got a source that tells me there was an operation set up to move meth north and cash south using two different welding trucks and two different drivers. Somebody grabbed the contents of one truck and left it up here, but the driver is still missing. Sounds like you found the other truck and maybe the other driver."

"Yeah, our guy down there said the Mexicans are still trying to ID the body but they were pretty sure it was a member of the Juarez Cartel. He had a pig face drawn on his forehead, which is a symbol the

Sinaloa Cartel uses to describe members of the Juarez Cartel."

"Was there anything inside the hidden compartment?" I asked.

"Not a damn thing."

CHAPTER FORTY
Counselor

"So, how does the doctor fit in?" Angie asked.

We had just finished clearing the dishes from her dining table, loading the dishwasher, and were getting ready to drive across town for a movie.

"I'm not sure if he fits in anywhere, except as another person on the list of people that Benny Shanks used his leverage on. The amount of money he owned Benny might have been enough to give him motive, but the way Benny was shot, and where he was shot, make it unlikely that Tyler Drake was the shooter."

"Let me change my shoes and I'll be ready," she said, heading off to the bedroom.

I was standing in the entryway and thinking about Dr. Drake when a vase on a table near the door caught my eye. I looked closer and realized that it was the same vase shattered when the wind caught it the night of Angie's cookout.

"Wow, you really got this put back together well," I said as she came out of the bedroom. "I can hardly tell it was broken."

"Luckily, most of the pieces were salvageable and it really wasn't that hard to put back together once I got started," she said.

I stood there staring at the vase

for a few seconds, as she opened the door and started out.

"Are you coming?" she asked, laughing.

"What? Oh, yeah," I said. "That just gave me an idea."

CHAPTER FORTY-ONE
bagel report

"Geez, I guess I'm glad you're not reporting this to me officially," Bob Clemmer said, after I briefed him on what I had learned so far. We were sitting at what had become our usual table at The Bagel Barn.

"I'd just as soon not have to tell the Chief right away that Dallas Jenkins' kid was mixed up in something with Benny Shanks," he continued. "The Chief and Dallas play golf together on a pretty regular basis."

"Well, it may not have anything to do with Benny's murder. It's still too early to tell," I said.

"And that's all I care about right now," he said. "Not that we would ignore a dope smuggling operation just because the Chief is buddies with somebody, but it sounds like the dope smuggling might have come to a stop without our involvement."

"By the way," I said. "Did you get any results back on that Texas Brain Freeze cup from the street where Benny was shot?"

"Not yet. The lab's so backed up right now it may be another week or two. I'd be surprised if they can get any prints off of it, but you never know."

"You may be right about Benny's death shutting down that smuggling operation," I said. "But somebody sure whacked a hornet's nest when they decided to take both the money and the load of meth it was supposed to pay for. They pissed off both sides and the middle and left all of the players suspecting each other."

"And we'll probably never know who the greedy party was. Not that it matters much," Clemmer said. "I don't care if they rip each other off all day long if it interrupts the flow of meth through Elmore."

"I understand," I said. "But I still need to find out what happened to Justin Ramey, and the only way to do that seems to be putting myself in the middle of these guys. And, there's always the chance it will lead me to who killed Benny."

"You really think your idea will work?" he said.

"I don't know but I won't know unless I try."

"You understand I can't sanction

what you're planning on doing. And, if something goes wrong you could end up getting yourself or somebody else killed. Not to mention the chance you could end up in jail or with a contract hit out on you. Those guys working for the Mexican drug cartels aren't anything like your average north-of-the-border knucklehead. There is absolutely no limit to what they will do to another human being if they consider them an enemy."

"I don't think the cartels care that much about a bunch of squabbling Americans," I said, hoping I knew what I was talking about.

"What about that second welding truck they found on the other side of the border with the chopped-up corpse?" he asked.

"Shane Gerber told me that the way they cut the guy up and left his body had all the hallmarks of the Sinaloa Cartel," I said. "I think Benny and his partners were moving meth from somebody competing with the Sinaloas. Reggie Marshall found out who it was and, after his guys hijacked the shipment they turned the truck and the driver over to the Sinaloas."

"Keeping the meth and the cash but letting the Sinaloas deal with the competition problem on their side of the border," Clemmer said.

"Right," I said. "Reggie probably does some business with them and handed the guy over as a favor."

"Pretty gruesome if Reggie knew what would happen to the guy."

"From what I hear Reggie Marshall's no slouch when it comes to dealing with his competitors," I said.

"But you don't like him for Benny's murder? That doesn't

make much sense."

"On the contrary," I said. "It wouldn't make much sense for Reggie to want to get rid of Benny, when Benny was the one he was trying to leverage by pulling off the heist in the first place. One load of dope and one bundle of cash is small potatoes compared to getting a piece of each shipment on a regular basis. Benny and Reggie are both old-school and Reggie knew he could count on Benny coming around and playing ball eventually."

"So, with Benny dead, if Reggie wants to restart the Juarez to Amarillo pipeline, he's forced to deal with who? Trey Jenkins? Or this Sammy Rosado guy?" Clemmer asked.

"Not Trey Jenkins," I said. "He's been spooked too badly at this point to want any more involvement in moving illegal drugs. And I don't know enough about Sammy Rosado to know if he would put the deal back together and let Reggie get his piece of it."

"Which brings us back to your plan," he said.

"Which brings us back to my plan."

"I guess all I can do is advise you not to go through with it. But, if it starts to go south I'll do what I can to help out."

"If it starts to go south there may not be time for you to help, but I appreciate the offer," I said, trying not to imagine all the different ways that things could go wrong with my plan.

CHAPTER FORTY-TWO
timmy and jimmy

I was walking back to my office from The Bagel Barn when my cell phone rang. I didn't recognize the number.

"Mr. Griffin? You may not remember me, but this is Maureen Wright."

"Of course, I remember you," I said. "Granny Mo, right?"

"That's right," she said with a chuckle. "Well, the reason I called is there's something going on over at the Ramey's trailer. There are a couple of men over there banging on the door and nobody's answering, but I know Courtney and the kids are in there."

"Do you recognize the men?" I asked.

"No, but I know they're not with the police. I know all the police in town."

I thanked her for calling as I was nearing my office and then instead of going inside, I got in my truck and drove to the Ramey's address. There were two men standing on the trailer's front porch and they turned to watch me when I pulled to the curb and parked. One of the men was Tim Kettle, who I'd caught watching me a few days earlier. Kettle's black pickup was parked behind the Ramey's pickup in the dirt driveway. The other guy was much larger and looked like he might not be as easy to push around as Kettle had been. As I walked up the driveway behind Kettle's pickup I noticed the tailgate had one of those chrome advertising emblems that car dealers put on the back of the vehicles they sell. Kettle's truck had come from a dealership in Amarillo.

"Tim Kettle," I said, giving him a friendly smile. "Here you are again. Why do I keep running into you?"

The bigger guy shot a questioning look at Kettle, who seemed embarrassed that I knew his name.

"Who is this," the big one asked, addressing Kettle.

"Some kind of private detective," Kettle mumbled.

"What are you guys doing here?" I asked, as if I'd caught them someplace they clearly shouldn't be.

"None of your business," the big one said, giving me his best stink-eye. "We don't have to talk to you."

"Oh, come on now," I said. "Is that really how Mr. Delano would expect you to behave when you come down here for a visit?"

"We don't--," Kettle started.

"Shut up!" the big one said, cutting him off. And then to me: "You don't know what you're talking about."

"Really?" I answered. "Frank Delano didn't send you down here to push people around to try to get his money back?"

"Okay, I think it's time for you to leave," the big one said, taking a step towards me.

I held up a hand.

"Hold on, I've got to take this," I said, reaching into my phone holster and pulling out my cell phone. I took another few steps as I looked down at the phone while they waited. When I was close enough, I held the phone up in the big one's face and snapped a picture, then swung it around to get one of Tim Kettle.

"Hey!" they yelled in unison.

"You can't do that," the big one said, reaching to take the phone away from me.

Even though he was bigger than Kettle, he was actually still a few inches shorter than me, so I stood my ground and held the phone up high with my right hand. When he made a lunging jump for it, moved it out of the way while simultaneously using my left hand to snatch his own phone from its holster on his right side. Once I had it I took a couple of quick steps to the back of Kettle's pickup and used the bumper to hop up into the bed. The big guy's face was so red it looked like his head was about to explode.

"Give that back you mother-fucker!" he said, standing with both hands on the side of the pickup bed.

"Get out of my damn truck," Kettle yelled.

I looked at his phone and brought up the list of contacts while I kept one eye on the big guy as he circled the pickup trying to decide on a plan of attack.

"Don't worry," I said. "I'll give it back. I just want to save us both some time and talk to Frank Delano directly."

"I hope you know you're making a big mistake," the big one said, circling to the back of the pickup and starting to hoist himself up on the bumper.

"Ah, here we go," I said, finding a

contact listed simply as *Frank* and hitting the *Dial* button.

As the big one swung a leg over the tailgate, I stepped up on the sidewall of the pickup bed and then up onto the top of the cab.

"Hey! Get the fuck down from there!" Kettle yelled.

My boots were making some scratches in the paint and some slight dents but nothing that a good paint and body man couldn't fix. The phone on the other end of the line was ringing as I watched the big one stand up in the pickup bed and start toward me. I let him get almost to me before sitting quickly at the front of the cab and then stepping down onto the hood. I tried to be careful but managed to break one of the windshield wipers in doing so. They really don't build trucks like they used to.

Someone at the other end of the

line finally picked up.

"Yeah?" It was a gruff voice, and slightly irritated.

I listened and waited as the big one started climbing up on the pickup cab. He was starting to breathe heavier from the exertion of literally throwing his weight around.

"Jimmy?" Delano said.

"No, Jimmy's a little busy right now," I said. "Can I have him call you back?"

"Who is this?" Delano asked, his voice moving from slightly irritated to really pissed off.

"I'm somebody you need to talk to, Frank," I said. "Is it okay to call you Frank?"

"Put Jimmy on," Delano said.

"Sorry, but we need to talk," I said. "I need to meet with you, either here or in Amarillo, it's your call."

"Meet with me? About what?"

"About why you sent Jimmy and Timmy down here in the first place," I said. "I've got some information you might be interested in."

"You still haven't told me who you are," he said. "I ain't got time to meet with just anybody."

"My name is Buddy Griffin," I said. "I think you probably already know I'm a private investigator, but what you don't know is that I can tell you what happened to that thing you lost and how you can go about getting it back. Or, maybe I should say *those things*. There were actually two things that went missing, weren't there?"

"I don't know what you're talking about. But, I know you used to be a cop, and I sure as hell ain't got time to meet with no damn cop."

Jimmy had finally gotten up on

the cab of the pickup and was starting to slide his legs down the windshield while Kettle stood by unsure of what to do. I hopped down off the pickup and started walking toward the street.

"Do you want to know what happened to your property or not?" I asked Delano.

He didn't say anything.

"Listen," I said. "You had a good thing going with Benny until this little hiccup. But, Benny's gone now and what I'm trying to tell you is I can help you get your property back and get things set up like they were before."

"Again officer, I don't know what you're talking about," he said.

"You're wasting your time waiting for Jimmy and Timmy to come up with something. I know exactly where the missing items are and how to get them back. Then, once that's all settled, things can pick up where they left off. There's still an enormous demand that isn't being met while we sit around talking in circles."

The line was silent for a few seconds before he responded. "You think I'm going to fall for some kind of entrapment setup? You must think I'm pretty stupid."

"Just meet with me and hear me out," I said. "You don't have to say a word if you don't want to."

I heard him sigh and mutter something I couldn't understand.

"Okay, fine," he said. "I got some time tomorrow afternoon after four. Give the phone to Jimmy and I'll have him write the address down for you."

CHAPTER FORTY-THREE
the lord is my jagermeister

As soon as I got the address from Jimmy, and Jimmy finally convinced Kettle that the two of them really couldn't do anything about the damage I'd inflicted on Kettle's pickup, they got in it and left. As I watched them drive off, I noticed Granny Mo sitting on her porch down the street. I waved and she gave me a thumbs-up signal. I heard the trailer door open behind me and Courtney

Ramey came out onto the trailer steps.

"Thank you," she said, as I approached. "I didn't know what to do about them and I was afraid they were going to break the door down or something."

"You're welcome," I said. "I've been meaning to stop by and ask you about something anyway. Do you mind if we go inside?"

"Uh, no, not at all," she said, looking a little flustered.

I started up the steps of the steel platform that served as a porch for the trailer as she opened the door and quickly stepped inside, shooting a quick glance around.

"I've got to apologize for how disorganized things is," she said. "I can't hardly keep up with the messes that boy of mine makes."

"Oh, it's no problem," I said, stepping inside and noticing

several empty beer cans and a microwave popcorn bag on the low bar that separated the kitchen from the living area. She motioned me towards a scarred beige leatherette couch while she quickly picked up the remote control and turned off the gigantic flat-screen television mounted on the opposite wall. The sound had already been muted, probably when Jimmy and Timmy started pounding on the door. On one side of the TV hung a mirror with the Jägermeister logo silkscreened on the surface and on the other side an arrangement of eight or ten decorative crosses.

"Now, what did you need to ask about?"

"Well, it's about Justin's phone," I said. "Remember how I told you we found it out in those sand dunes near that welding truck?"

"Uh-huh," she said.

"I may not have mentioned it at the time, but the phone still worked after we found it. They had to recharge the battery, but it worked just fine. So, I got to checking the call history and missed calls and messages that were left for that phone. But what was strange was that there were only five messages waiting on Justin's voicemail when I checked. There were a couple from Benny and the other three were from you. And, what seems even stranger is that all of them were left between Thursday morning and Friday morning. But you were expecting Justin to be home early Wednesday morning after he finished making that run with the welding truck on Tuesday night."

"Well, he wasn't even supposed to take a phone with him," she said. "I didn't want to call and make it ring at the wrong time. That would have gotten him in trouble."

"I can understand that," I said. "So, you waited to see if Justin would come home later in the day on Wednesday, and he didn't. And so maybe you thought he'd come home in the middle of the night on Wednesday, so you'd wait a little longer. Then, you get to Thursday morning and you decide that it doesn't matter if it gets him in trouble or not, you've got to at least try to reach him."

"I had to know what was going on," she said. "I knew something was definitely wrong at that point."

"So, you call, but the call goes directly to voicemail, so you leave a message. And, when he doesn't call back, you leave another message a few hours later. But, he doesn't call back and doesn't come home all day Thursday, so you call again and leave another message on Friday morning. And, Benny was still trying to get ahold of him too. He called Thursday night and again early on Friday morning, a few hours before you left the last message. But, one thing I couldn't figure out was why there weren't any more messages after the one you left on Friday morning. Why wouldn't you keep trying to get a message to Justin, to find out where he was?"

"Cause I knew I didn't need to," she said, her eyes wide. "I already left three messages before. He would have got those if he was going to get any of them."

"Maybe," I allowed. "But, why would Benny stop leaving messages about the same time too?"

"I don't know," she said, standing up and moving around the living room, straightening a knit throw on the back of a chair and then stepping over to the kitchen to clear the beer cans and empty microwave popcorn bag off the bar.

"Is it because you heard from Justin on Friday morning?" I asked. "Maybe you knew where he was, and maybe Benny knew too? Neither one of you needed to keep calling that cell phone to leave messages, because you already knew where he was."

"That's not... Wait a minute," she said. "That's crazy. I came to see you at your office after that. Why would I do that if I already knew where Justin was?"

"Here's what I think happened," I said. "Somebody ran Justin down in that welding truck, probably shooting at him the whole way. Somehow, he escaped, but the people chasing him got away with whatever it was he was hauling in that truck. Now Justin might not have known exactly what he was hauling, but he knew enough to know that people would be upset when it got stolen. So, he hid out for a couple of days, and then he finally called you or he called Benny. I'm guessing maybe both of you. Maybe he talked to Benny and told him what happened and Benny told him to lay low until he could straighten things out. After all, Benny got Justin the job driving the truck and some of the people involved might suspect that Justin and Benny decided to stage some kind of robbery to keep whatever was in that truck for themselves. Then, the very next night, before he can figure out how to fix things, Benny gets shot, leaving Justin in limbo with nobody he can trust to believe his side of the story. I think you came to me to help with your cover story that Justin had disappeared and was still missing. How am I doing, so far?"

"None of that is true," she said. She wasn't a very good liar.

"I need to talk to Justin," I said. "He needs help right now, and I think you know that. Those two idiots I just chased off aren't the only people looking for him and the sooner I talk to him the sooner we can figure out how to get this straightened out. He can't hide out forever, and he's in serious danger if the people looking for him find him before I do."

I got up from the couch and stood across the bar from her.

She looked at me and shook her head.

"I really didn't know where he was," she said. "Benny came to see me on Friday morning. He said

Justin was okay, but he had lost his phone. He said that Justin couldn't come home right away but he would tell Justin to call me. Benny said it was important that I just act like everything was okay and wait to hear from Justin. But, then Benny got shot and I didn't ever hear from Justin, so I came to see you."

"Did Justin ever call?" I asked.

She didn't answer.

"Tell him I need to talk to him," I said. I'll meet him anywhere."

CHAPTER FORTY-FOUR
transmission man

Driving from Elmore up to Amarillo the next day, I hoped Frank Delano would buy into the story I was about to tell him. It was part of a loosely-scripted plan I laid out for Bob Clemmer earlier. From what I had learned so far, I knew there were people on both ends of the drug transaction that were looking for Justin Ramey, and the only way I could keep him alive was to get closer to the parties involved and try to influence their actions. And, I hoped to do so by trying to insert myself into the spot that Benny Shanks had occupied in the connection between Sammy Rosado and Frank Delano. If I could buy time for Justin and find out more about what led to Benny Shanks murder it would be worth it. The meeting with Delano was risky, especially since I didn't have anything concrete to offer, but I figured I could wing it if any questions came up that I didn't anticipate.

The address that Delano's guy Jimmy had given me led to a transmission shop in the south part of town, sandwiched between a lumber yard and a self-storage place. A woman was sitting at a desk in the reception area talking on the phone. When she finished, I told her who I was there to see and she led me through the garage bays to a small suite of offices at the other end of the building.

Unlike Sandy Doyle, Frank Delano didn't look anything like a drug kingpin, at least not the way they look on TV and in the movies. He looked more like a guy who might be good with a wrench, figured out that fixing transmissions wasn't going to make him a millionaire, and decided to take a different route. But, I've learned that you can't always judge how dangerous a man is by his initial appearances. And, the fact that Trey Jenkins' house had been burned down told me something about how seriously he took the situation with the missing money and meth.

I didn't see Tim Kettle anywhere around, but his sidekick Jimmy was there and made a show of searching me for weapons or wires before he let me get too close to

Delano. Once that was out of the way, he ushered me into Delano's office. Delano gestured for me to sit while Jimmy took up a position blocking the doorway, as if his job was to keep me from jumping up and running out of there.

"Jimmy, give us a few minutes, would you?" Delano said, pointing to the door. Jimmy looked hurt but stepped out of the office and closed the door behind him.

"Okay," Delano said. "Here we are. What was it you had to say?"

"It's real simple, and you know I'm not wearing a wire, so I'm just going to put it out there." I said. "You had a pretty smooth operation going with Benny Shanks before things got interrupted. I think I know what happened and what it will take to put things right. I can work it so the product gets delivered to you and the money gets delivered to the people down south."

"Like I told you on the phone, you must think I'm pretty stupid. I don't care if you're not wearing a wire or not. I don't have any idea what you're talking about."

"I understand," I said. "You don't know me at all, and I walk in here talking about things that I'm not supposed to know anything about. But, figuring things out is what I do. I did it for over twenty years as a cop, and now I'm working for myself. And, for you, if you'll listen."

"I'm listening."

"The way I see it," I said. "You got some things missing, which is bad. But, worse than losing the money and product was losing the setup you had with Benny. The income stream. And, with all due respect, you were so busy looking at one little tree that you totally missed the forest. The missing meth and cash were just a couple of trees in this magnificent forest you had right in front of you. But, instead of concentrating on fixing the problem and getting the income stream going again, you sent Jimmy and Timmy down to Elmore to try to flush out whoever hijacked the goods. Now Benny's dead, which you may or may not have some involvement in, and Benny's partner, whose background in the oil business is pretty crucial to the operation, is too scared to even think of getting involved again. Did you really think you would get results by burning down this kid's house?"

"Let's get one thing straight," he said. "I didn't have nothing to do with what happened to Benny."

I shrugged.

"I'll take your word for it," I said. "Not important to me now. What is important is that I think I know what happened to the meth and the money, and I think I can put the operation together again and fix the problem that caused this interruption."

"You *think* you can? You *think* you can? Like I said, I don't know what you're talking about. But if I did, do you think I would've agreed to let you waste my time by telling me what you *think* you can do?"

"Well, anything I do depends on whether you'll agree to go along," I said. "It all hinges on you. I wanted to come here first, out of respect to you, to get your blessing before I start putting this together. I didn't think it would be right to try to set something up with the assumption that you'd go along with it."

He looked at me for a few seconds and then balled his fist and then brought a thick index finger down to press against the surface of his desk.

"I'm not saying I agree to anything, you understand? I ain't gonna buy no pig in a poke."

"But, you'll at least agree to listen to the details if I can put something together? And, you'll keep Jimmy and Timmy busy doing other things until I can get back with you?" I asked.

He looked at me stone-faced and nodded.

"I'll give you that."

"And one more thing," I said. "Justin, the kid Jimmy and Timmy were looking for, he didn't have anything to do with what happened. He didn't even know what he was moving. So, I need your assurance that it's safe for him to come back home."

He shrugged again.

"Long as you're taking full responsibility for putting things right, I got no problem with that."

CHAPTER FORTY-FIVE
lime green

Leaving Delano's shop, I still wasn't sure how my visit might help me figure out who murdered Benny Shanks, but at least now I was a little better acquainted with one of the key players, and I knew that just trying to insert myself into the situation might be enough to make something pop.

I decided to stop for lunch before leaving Amarillo, so I pulled into an old west themed barbecue joint with about a dozen cars in the parking lot. I picked up a copy of a local classified ad newspaper in the entryway and got a booth by a window. After I ordered, I was skimming the antique section of the paper, hoping to find a bargain on an early Victrola, when I was distracted by a car in the parking lot. Now, I've never really been much of a car guy, but I've always liked the muscle cars of the 1970's and I was excited to see the car makers start making modern versions of some of the old classics, even if I'll probably never buy one for myself. They're always fun to look at, and I especially like the current Dodge Challenger and how much it resembles the earlier version.

That's why I honed in on the new lime green Challenger with black hood stripes as it slowly rolled through the restaurant parking lot before pulling back onto the street. As it paused at the parking lot exit I noticed it had a Missouri vanity plate that read "TT4". It disappeared on down the street and I didn't think anything more about it until two hours later when I noticed a Challenger with the same paint colors in my rear-view mirror when I was coming through Lubbock. But even then, I didn't think about it being the same car. There are a lot of those new Challengers around, and this one was too far back to tell whether the front license plate was from Missouri or Texas.

However, later that afternoon, when I glanced out my office window and saw a lime green Challenger parked in the auxiliary courthouse parking lot two blocks away, I decided there might be somebody following me.

Sometimes I'm a regular Lieutenant Columbo about these things. I puzzled over what to do for a few minutes before deciding it was time to go back to school.

Starcher County Community College was a cluster of buildings located just off the Andrews Highway a couple of miles outside of town. The campus was laid out with a dozen buildings in the center and a wide drive that made a complete circle around the campus. The circle drive could only be accessed from one road leading in from the highway. Any visitor to the College had to turn off the highway, drive a couple hundred yards to the circle drive, turn left or right, and then drive to one of the half dozen parking lots between the circle drive and the buildings in the center of the campus. I had never actually attended class at SCCC but had been to enough basketball games and college rodeo events over the years that I was familiar with the layout.

As I headed out of town I kept watching my mirror for the flash of green I expected to show up but got almost to the College entrance before it appeared. I turned into the entrance and slowed down a little, but not enough to make it obvious that I was waiting for the Challenger to catch up. I turned right and started around the circle and was almost halfway around before I could tell that the Challenger had done the same. At this point, I sped up a bit until I was situated with a building between us and quickly pulled into the parking lot next to the gymnasium and parked next to a cargo van in such a way that my pickup was hidden from the circle drive. I watched the Challenger roll past and waited until it was out of sight before pulling back out onto the circle drive going the opposite direction. I rolled along slowly, giving the Challenger time to complete the circle and pass its only escape route — the road that lead back to the highway.

Then, we were rolling towards each other, both still observing the posted 15 mph speed limit of the circle drive. I was trying to decide whether I would wave or honk or both when we passed, but the Challenger quickly darted into one of the parking lots, leaving me out on the circle drive my myself. I continued on toward the exit road as I watched the Challenger roll slowly through the parking lot, passing up dozens of perfectly good parking places, obviously killing time and pretending to belong there. It was a Monday, but it was late in the day, so there weren't many cars on campus besides ours. I slowed when I reached the exit road, turned onto it, rolled a few feet and stopped. Then, I put the transmission in "Park", turned off the engine, and waited.

It was less than a quarter of a mile from the parking lot where the Challenger was hiding to the exit road where I was parked, and the terrain was flat and mostly treeless. If the person driving the Challenger was watching me, they would know that the only way off the campus was to drive past where I was parked. I rolled my window down and enjoyed the relative quiet of the campus setting. Even though the Challenger was some distance away, I could still make out the low rumble of its engine. After a few seconds, I heard the engine give a low growl as the driver gave it a little gas after parking in a space roughly facing where I sat. Then the Challenger engine quit and I settled in for a wait.

I turned the radio on low and found a baseball game, hoping the drone of the announcers didn't put me to sleep as quickly as it did when I listened at home on the couch. It always struck me as funny how different the soundtracks to televised sporting events were. Golf tournaments were quiet and the announcers practically whispered their delivery, while football broadcasts turned up the crowd noise so loud that the hosts had to shout so much they were probably hoarse the next day. Baseball occupied sort of a middle ground.　There was crowd noise, but it was kept low enough that the announcers could speak at a conversational level, except during a big play.

It took less than an inning of the Texas Rangers at bat against the Washington Nationals before I heard the rumble of the Challenger's engine as it fired up again.　I watched through my side mirror as the driver threw it in gear and began rolling out of the parking lot.　I unholstered and checked my gun while I waited, watching the Challenger turn onto the exit road and pull up beside me.　The passenger window rolled down and a muscular thirtyish man with close-cropped dark hair and sunglasses leaned over the center console toward me.

"You ready to get this over with?" he yelled.

"It's your call," I said.

He looked at me for a second and then nodded and gestured for me to lead the way. "After you, cowboy."

CHAPTER FORTY-SIX
scouting party

I led the guy in the Challenger back into town and parked on the street in front of Lita's Little Mexico. The Challenger parked a couple of spaces down. Probably didn't want those doors dinged by careless diners. The driver was taller than I expected when he unfolded himself from the Challenger's cockpit and followed me around the end of the building to my office door. More muscular than I expected too. I was glad he hadn't suggested a wrestling match. At least not yet.

I unlocked the door, ushered him in and gestured towards a chair.

"By the way, I'm Buddy Griffin," I said, offering a handshake.

"Carter Branch," he said, somewhat cautiously shaking hands.

"Tell me, Carter. What made you want to follow me all the way down here from Amarillo?"

"What exactly is it you do?" he said, looking around at my office and helping himself to a business card from a holder on my desk.

"Private Investigations?" he asked, reading the card before slipping it in his shirt pocket. "What, like Magnum P.I. or something like that?"

"Yeah, something like that," I said. "And, if your name is Carter Branch, then why the TT4 on your license plate?"

"Ah, oh that. All the good license plate combinations using C and B were already taken. Now, what kind of private investigator has an office inside a Mexican food restaurant? Do you own the restaurant too? Just do the private eye bit on the side?"

"Do you even have Mexican food up there in Missouri, or do you mostly eat fried squirrel and other varmints?" I said.

He actually smiled at that one.

"Funny," he said. "But, don't knock squirrel if you haven't tried it."

"Come on," I said. "Really. What are you doing down here?"

He looked around the office again and sighed.

"Just trying to get the lay of the land," he said. "Only I can't quite figure out where you fit in."

"What do you mean?" I asked.

"Well, from what my sources tell me, you've always been a Boy Scout," he said. "A decorated member of the Austin Police Department for what, over twenty years? With no obvious evidence that you were on the take, or ever involved in anything questionable. Then, you retire and move up here. Back to where you grew up. And decide to make up for lost time by running drugs while you pretend to be a private investigator? It kind of makes sense, though. It's always those straight arrow cops who turn out to be really dirty when you peel back a few layers."

"I'm impressed," I said. "You've done some homework."

"Like I told you, I'm just trying to fit it all together," he said. "Like that guy in Amarillo. Delano? How'd you get him roped into this?

I mean the guy's probably done a few questionable transmission overhauls and padded some repair bills over the years, but I can't find any sign that he's done anything really bad since he got out of juvie back in 1979."

Before I could say anything else, Norris Jackson stuck his head in the door.

"Is this a bad time?" he asked, seeing the guest chair in front of my desk occupied.

"No, not at all," I said. "Come on in. Sheriff Norris Jackson, I'd like you to meet Carter Branch. Mr. Branch is down here from Missouri to sample some of our regional cuisine."

They shook hands and Norris sat down beside Carter and then passed a sheet of paper over to me.

"Here's that thing you called

about earlier," he said.

I scanned the page and then looked at Carter.

"Who is Eli Treviso? That your real name?"

He looked at me for a beat.

"No, not me. I'm just driving his car."

"You got any ID on you?" Norris asked.

"Why, am I under arrest or something?"

Norris looked at me. "Should I arrest him?"

I shrugged. "I guess not. I don't know that he's done anything wrong except waste some of my time. Follows me down here from Amarillo and then won't give me a straight answer about anything."

"Want me to handcuff him and rough him up a little?" Norris asked. "See if he comes around?"

"Naw, you're not really any good

at that," I said. "Besides, he's probably got a good twenty pounds of muscle on you, and he looks like he's fifteen years younger and in better shape."

"Yeah, but I've got my handcuffs right here. And, I could tase him if he resists."

Carter shook his head. "Do you guys do stand-up comedy in here after they serve the sopapillas?"

"Come on Carter," I said. "You said you're here to find out what's going on and where I fit in. Why don't we both just lay it all out there and let Norris get back to writing speeding tickets?"

Carter looked at Norris and then at me.

"Yeah, okay. I guess."

I looked at Norris and then pointed at the door.

"What? That means I've got to leave?" Norris whined. "That's not quite fair."

"Catch you later Norris," I said.

"Is that guy really the Sheriff?" Carter asked after Norris left.

"He really is," I said. "You want something to drink before we get started?"

"What have you got?"

Half an hour later we were each on our second Shiner Bock but hadn't gotten down to business yet. We had talked about oil wells and I had explained why people would want to live in the middle of a landscape that looked so desolate when compared to other parts of the country.

"What makes you think I'm involved in drug trafficking?" I finally asked. "And, more importantly, how do I know that you aren't?"

He sighed and thought about it for a few seconds.

"Okay, I guess if it's time to level, I'll go first," he said. He took another pull on his beer and set the bottle down.

"The guy who owns that car I'm driving is named Eli Trevisi. He owns a trucking company in Kansas City called Trevisi Transport. The company has been around forever. They haul all sorts of stuff, for all sorts of customers. Sometimes it's a full load of something for one customer and sometimes they carry stuff for two or three customers on the same truck. Anyway, a few weeks back, a driver was making a run from Phoenix to the Northeast when he keeled over dead while eating supper at a truck stop in Rolla, Missouri. Face first into his mashed potatoes."

"Those starches will kill you," I said.

"Tell me about it," he said. "Anyway, this happened on a weekend, and when they contacted the office, Eli happens to take the call. He sends one of his best guys out to find the truck, do a quick inventory, and finish the run. So, this guy gets there and finds some extra freight that isn't on the manifest. He calls Eli, and Eli sends me out there since I'm closer to Rolla than he is."

"If Eli's in Kansas City, then where were you?" I asked.

"Lake of the Ozarks. About the middle of the state. So, I go to Rolla and the guy shows me a stack of insulation panels on a pallet. We call Eli and he tells the guy to unload it there and I sit with it until Eli can send another truck to pick it up. They take this stack of panels back to one of Trevisi Transport's long-term storage warehouses in Kansas City and hold it there, thinking somehow it got on the wrong truck and things will sort themselves out. But, nobody ever reports anything missing from a shipment and nobody calls to ask where their insulation panels are."

"That kind of thing happen a lot?"

"No, but stuff does get misrouted or stolen in transport. Eli doesn't let it go, though. He's starting to wonder if maybe some of his people are using his trucks to transport loads and collecting payment for it off the books. Then he decides to take a closer look at the pallet of insulation panels, so he goes out to the long-term warehouse, where nobody ever goes, and he finds the pallet. These insulation panels are all wrapped in layers of that polyethylene stretch film, so Eli cuts through all that, starts separating the panels and finds a big hollowed out area filled with plastic-wrapped bricks of something that Eli knows isn't legal. He calls in some help and they test what's inside the bricks without leaving any evidence that they looked at them and find out it's meth. They repack everything, stretch-wrap it just like it was, and move the pallet to the main Trevisi warehouse, where it sits in plain sight for a few days. Then, poof! It disappears in the middle of the night."

"Who took it?" I asked.

"No clue."

"Security cameras?"

"They missed it. When Eli went back to look at the footage there were half-hour gaps in the coverage throughout the day. Whoever took the pallet was either really smart or really lucky."

"So, you don't know where it ended up. Where was the original driver headed when he made his final stop in Rolla?"

"Baltimore, but he had stops in Indianapolis and Columbus on the way."

"And, there's no way to know for sure where the dope was headed," I said.

"No, that's why Eli decided to put me on figuring out where it came from."

"So, how did you know the connection to Delano's transmission shop?"

"The truck had a GPS tracker that records its route with a time stamp so you can see where it has been at any point. I just traced it back from Rolla to the shop in Amarillo. The trip history showed the driver was only there for a few minutes but it was long enough to make me want to stop and give it a look."

"When Eli found the dope, why didn't he just call the police and let them take care of it?"

He took a swig to drain the last of his beer and held the empty bottle up. I got two more from the office fridge.

"A couple of reasons. First, the driver was an old friend of Eli's and he couldn't believe the guy would willingly put Eli's business at risk by transporting dope."

"Yeah, but still. It just seems like calling in law enforcement would have been the sensible thing to do."

"The main thing you gotta understand about Eli is that he grew up in the trucking business and he's been able to keep the doors open in good times and bad. Overall, he's an honest businessman who keeps his word and never tries to screw his customers."

He paused, took a drink and seemed lost in his thoughts.

"But?" I said.

"But what?"

"You were leading up to something," I said.

"I guess what I was leading up to was that sometimes even an honest businessman has to bend the rules a little bit. When he found the meth, he couldn't be sure how it would play out if he called in the cops. So, he decided to try to find out as much as he could on his own."

"He didn't want to step on any toes before he knew whose toes they were," I said.

"You might say that. Trevisi Transport has been around a long time, and Eli's made some acquaintances over the years that aren't one hundred percent above-board. He just wanted to find out who all was involved in putting that stuff on his trucks before he took any action."

I was getting the feeling that Eli did more than bend a few rules, and that he might have more to hide from the authorities than Carter was letting on.

"How long have you worked for Eli?" I asked.

"How long? That's kind of complicated."

"How so?"

He focused on slowly peeling the paper label off of his beer bottle.

"My dad drove a truck for Eli's dad when I was little. He was driving a Trevisi truck when he was killed in a botched hijacking when I was ten years old. Eli was about the same age as my dad and didn't have any sons, so he kind of took care of me. My mom pretty much checked out after Dad got killed. She stayed drunk or high most of the time and went from one loser boyfriend to the next. Eli kept tabs on me and always made sure I stayed out of trouble and had some kind of stability by giving me a job helping out around the Trevisi warehouse. He'd take me on vacation to his house at Lake of the Ozarks with the rest of his family and treated me like I was his own son."

"Did you say you live at the lake now?"

"Yeah. When I came back from Afghanistan Eli gave me a job working at Trevisi Transport, but that didn't work out. He was having some renovations done on his house at the lake and needed somebody to be there to oversee the work and take care of things, so I moved into one of the guest rooms there. I had actually lived at the lake house before, during the summers when I was in high school and college, working at a few of the restaurants and bars around the lake. Eli knows a lot of people in Kansas City that have pretty nice houses on the lake, so he started spreading the word that I was available to keep an eye on their places and take care of things when they were away. Pretty soon I had half a dozen houses that I watched and took care of when the owners were away. Eli helped me get set up as a business and let me live in his house there until I got my feet on the ground."

He reached in his back pocket for his wallet and pulled out a dog-eared business card. He held it up just long enough for me to read

"The House Guy" with his name below, and an address in Osage Beach, Missouri, before tucking it back into his wallet.

"But Eli still calls on you when he needs you to what, use the skills you picked up in Afghanistan?"

He smiled.

"Yeah, something like that. He knows he can trust me, and that I can maintain my cool under pressure."

"When things get messy," I said.

"Oh, I try to keep things clean," he said, laughing. "But I'm about all talked out. I think it's your turn to spill the beans about what you're doing in the middle of all of this."

"Fair enough," I said.

I wasn't sure how much I could trust Carter Branch yet, or if he was being straight with me about where Trevisi Transport fit into the picture, but I knew I wouldn't get anywhere if I didn't at least share a little information in return.

I gave him a rundown of most of what I knew about the meth transport setup, Justin Ramey's disappearance and Benny Shanks' murder. I left out the part about my recent contact with Justin. I also left out my working theory that Reggie Marshall might have something to do with the welding truck incident and Benny's murder.

"If I understand what you're saying, Benny Shanks and his crew picked the stuff up south of here and then handed it off to Delano in Amarillo," he said, after I finished.

"That's right," I said. "And I think Delano's guys must have taken the bricks out of the welding truck and hidden them in the insulation panels that your driver picked up. There was a lumber yard next door to the transmission shop. Maybe that ties in somehow."

"That would make sense," he said. "Transport the stuff part of the way using the welding trucks and then change the way it's packaged for the rest of the trip. Adds another level of security."

"What do you do now?" I asked. "Benny Shanks was the one responsible for setting up the pipeline to Amarillo. Now that he's gone and your wayward trucker is dead, isn't the problem taken care of?"

"I guess that will be up to Eli. I'll tell him what I've found out and see what he wants me to do."

CHAPTER FORTY-SEVEN
show me

A couple of days later I met with Bob Clemmer over beers at a little bar that a retired Elmore cop had opened up on the outskirts of town. We had talked on the phone after my run-in with Carter Branch, and Clemmer wanted to meet after tracking down more information on the new parties I had told him about.

He slid a large envelope across the table to me.

"Carter Branch came back clean,

and the military background checks out. Went to Afghanistan, spent about eight years there, including some time as an MP, then was discharged. He seemed to fall off the grid for about four years after that and then shows up in Kansas City working for Trevisi Transport for a few months. Then he moves to someplace called Osage Beach, which is on that Lake of the Ozarks you mentioned. He's got a business license for a company called The House Guy, LLC. The organization papers were filed by a high dollar law firm in Kansas City."

"What do you make of the missing four years after he left the military," I asked.

"Seems odd," he admitted. "It's pretty hard to stay invisible for very long in the United States, but maybe he wasn't in the country for all that time."

"What do you mean?" I asked.

"I know a guy with an intelligence background and I ran Carter Branch's information by him. He was able to look at the military side of his records and said Branch could have spent those missing years working for the CIA or one of those quasi-governmental groups that operate in the Middle East, doing black-ops shit. Branch had the kind of training and skills the spooks look for to handle that kind of job."

"And what about the story Branch gave me about why he followed me down here."

"No way to know how true it is," he said. "But I couldn't verify the part about the truck driver dying at a diner near Rolla, Missouri."

"And Eli Trevisi and his trucking business?" I asked. "Any chance they would have been on the receiving end of the meth Benny was shipping north?"

"Trevisi's operation currently seems pretty clean from what I can tell. I did find some evidence that Trevisi's old man may have had some mob connections in the 1960's but back then that wasn't uncommon in the trucking industry. Now, Eli himself got into some trouble when he was going to college in Dallas. And, that's where it starts to get a little more interesting."

"How so?"

"Well, Eli picked up a stolen property charge and ended up doing three years at Huntsville instead of finishing his college degree."

"Following in his mobster father's footsteps?" I said.

"Looks like he was headed that direction for a while anyway. But that's not the most interesting part. I remembered seeing a stint at Huntsville on Benny Shanks sheet. So, I checked and sure enough, Benny Shanks and Eli Trevisi were both guests of the State of Texas at the Huntsville Unit at the same time."

"It just gets curiouser and curiouser, doesn't it?" I said.

CHAPTER FORTY-EIGHT
benny, eli and benny

Benny's Pawn and Loan looked more like a daycare center when I walked in two days later. Two six-year-old girls were re-arranging the items displayed on the floor of the pawn shop, while three younger boys were playing chase around the counters and display cases.

Maria Schankowitz was talking on a cell phone while pulling a fourth boy away from an air compressor he was examining. I gravitated towards the gun display while she wrapped up her conversation and met me.

"You're back," she said. "Looking for a good deal on a gun? We've got a lot to choose from."

I asked to look at a Smithfield Armory 1911 pistol that was displayed in a fancy after-market presentation case. I didn't really need to add to my small gun collection unless it was something I could use in my work, but the 1911 was pretty nice.

"That came from a woman that lived down the street from us whose husband was a gun nut," she said. "He died a while back and she didn't know what to do with all the guns, so Benny helped her out by taking some of them and finding buyers for the rest."

"That was nice," I said. "Oh, by the way, have you ever heard of a guy named Eli Trevisi?"

"Eli? Of course. We've been friends with Eli and Shauna forever. We used to go to Las Vegas with them all the time."

"Really?"

"Oh, yeah. When we started out, we always had to stay downtown at the Horseshoe. My Benny was good friends with Benny Binion, so everything was always comped and my Benny and Eli would hang out with Benny Binion while Shauna and I would go shopping. After Benny Binion died and they built The Mirage we started staying there, which was closer to the shopping mall."

"Have you talked to Eli since Benny passed?" I asked.

"Oh, yeah. He was one of the first people I called. He and Benny were really close. Did you know they were in Huntsville together?"

"Really? When was that?"

"Oh, God, I don't know. Ages ago. It wasn't Benny's first time in prison, but it was Eli's. I think Eli was in there for stolen property or something. He was just a college kid without much experience at that sort of thing. But, Eli was smart and could talk his way out of just about anything."

"Anyway, one day in the yard, Benny does something to disrespect somebody in one of the gangs, and they almost killed Benny right on the spot. But, Eli happens to be standing nearby and speaks up and uses his smarts to convince these gang members that Benny didn't mean any harm and it would be better for them in the long run to just let whatever Benny did pass."

"Well, those gang members didn't know what to think of this scrawny college kid sticking his nose in, but they listened, and Benny was able to walk away in one piece. We all laughed about that for years, how big bad Benny Schankowitz needed college boy Eli to save him. But, it was that one incident that led to their friendship. After that Benny took Eli under his wing a little bit and they watched out for each other. It wasn't too long after that some big White Power dude decided he wanted to make Eli his bitch. Benny never talked about the details of what happened, but the guards found the White Power dude dead, and nobody else ever bothered Eli after that. I don't know whether Eli had something to do with it, or Benny, or both of them. The guy didn't die of old age though."

"After he got out, Benny never stayed in contact with anybody else he was inside with, except for Eli," she said. "And, Eli took it pretty hard when I told him about Benny getting shot."

"Do you think Benny and Eli might have been in business together? In the part of the business that Benny didn't tell you about?"

"I could be wrong, but I really don't think so," she said. "I heard Benny offer to cut him in on some things over the years, and Eli always turned him down. Politely, though. Now, don't get the wrong idea. Eli was no choir boy. I just don't think he ever wanted to take the chance that some kind of business deal might screw up their friendship."

CHAPTER FORTY-NINE
no habla

Sammy Rosado's bar was called The Ramp, and it was located on the east side of Del Rio, on the highway that led to Laughlin Air Force Base. When I stepped inside, I wasn't too surprised to find it drew heavily on the military aviation theme, from the hangar-like building design, to the Air Force memorabilia on the walls, and the drink names on the menu like Stick Landing and Charlie Foxtrot.

It was late afternoon, but the happy hour crowd hadn't arrived yet, so I sat at the bar and ordered a beer while I looked around. The bartender was busy stocking the bar while one waitress took care of the patrons sitting at tables and delivered food orders from the back.

I caught the bartender's attention.

"Is Sammy around?"

"I'm not sure. I haven't seen him yet." he said, involuntarily glancing at the door leading to the back. He quickly went back to washing bar glasses.

"Would you mind checking to see if he's back there?" I said, holding out a business card. "Tell him we have a mutual friend in Elmore."

The bartender picked up a phone and punched in a number. He spoke in Spanish, probably thinking I wouldn't understand when he told Sammy what I had told him, and added that I looked like I might be a cop. He hung up and Sammy came through the door from the back a few seconds later.

"How can I help you?" he said, choosing to remain behind the bar with the bartender, who acted like he wasn't eavesdropping while he polished the draft beer faucets.

"Is there some place a little more private we can talk?" I said. "I'm a friend of Trey Jenkins."

He hesitated for a second before telling the bartender in Spanish to let Gonzalo know to be ready.

Then, he came out from behind the bar and led me to another area of the bar that was closed off by a heavy dark velvet drape. He turned on a bank of lights and motioned me to a table at the far end of the space.

"I'll be right with you," he said, disappearing behind the other side of the curtain.

A few seconds later, a husky bouncer-type that I assumed was Gonzalo came in and subjected me to a quick pat-down and measured dose of intimidation. When he was satisfied that I wasn't packing and was sufficiently in awe of his might, he left and Sammy returned.

"I'm sorry about that," he said, as we sat down at the table. "Now, what's this about?"

"Let me start by assuring you that I'm not a cop," I said. "I used to be, but I'm not anymore. I know some things about your situation, and I'm just asking for you to hear me out before you say anything."

I told him that I knew all about his partnership with Benny and Trey and how Sammy was the one that had arranged to have the welding trucks built. And, that I knew about the hijacking of the welding trucks and that drugs and money were both missing. He listened and watched me, careful not to agree to anything or offer any comments.

"Back when I was a cop," I said. "They used to call me 'Bloodhound' around the office because I was so good at sniffing out the clues that helped us solve murders. Like I said, I'm not a cop anymore, but it's hard to turn a nose like this one off. I started looking into the disappearance of this kid who was driving one of those welding trucks and it led me right into the middle of this mess that you've been dealing with."

"Frankly, I was surprised to find you still alive," I said. "The fact that you're still upright and breathing air must mean the guys on your end of the deal have a soft spot for you. Either that, or you make them so much money in other areas that they give you some leeway when it comes to losses."

"Anyway, long story short, I know what happened to the contents of both trucks that night and I can help you get it back."

He started to answer, but I held up a hand.

"I don't want you to say a word right now. Just think about what I said and be willing to listen some more once I iron out all of the details. And, if you think I'm jerking your chain just give Trey a call. He knows I'm putting something together to fix what got broken."

With that, I stood up and walked out, giving Gonzalo a wink as I

walked past.

CHAPTER FIFTY
huevos malo

There were still a couple of hours of daylight left when I walked out of The Ramp, so I decided to get a little closer to my next destination and overnighted at a motel on the outskirts of San Antonio. I slept pretty well despite the truck noise from the interstate and a group of rowdy kids in the room above mine.

The greasy spoon attached to the motel served a mediocre version of huevos rancheros for breakfast, with some type of picante sauce from a jar thrown on top of a scoop of canned refried beans and two over-cooked eggs. I guess I've become spoiled by the cooking at Lita's.

After breakfast, I got back on the road, but was in no particular hurry to arrive in Houston too early in the day. The windshield time allowed me to think things through and further analyze my strategy. My biggest worry in trying to insert myself into the middle of the situation is that one of the parties would get the idea that I had some involvement in the hijacking, since I had already told Frank Delano that I could replace what had been stolen. Even though I hadn't spelled it out that way to Sammy Rosado, if Sammy talked to Frank Delano, the two of them might decide to come after me the same way Delano had gone after Trey Jenkins. I was counting on all of the parties being so distrustful of the others that they wouldn't share information.

I just hoped I turned out to be right about that.

CHAPTER FIFTY-ONE
sticky wicket

Reggie Marshall's office looked like it belonged in an episode of *Pimp My Pimp's Crib*. It was located in an otherwise unremarkable office building that resembled a data processing center, situated not far from a Houston freeway interchange. But, inside there was some expensive looking art on the wall, and there was the added cache' of an attractive receptionist named Chloe with pale blue hair and an

Australian accent. Chloe took my name and recited a short list of unconventional office refreshments, including guava juice and spearmint tea. I declined all and sat on an expensive leather couch thumbing through a copy of The Robb Report while I waited to be summoned.

As Chloe ushered me into his office, Reggie Marshall sat at a highly-polished table made of some type of exotic wood that was undoubtedly purchased on the black market after being harvested illegally from a rainforest somewhere. Reggie was wearing an expensive tailored suit and a gold chain heavy enough to shame any of the first-generation rappers that made it onto MTV during the 1980's. Aside from the wood of the table, almost everything else in the room was made of glass or plated in gold. Even the huge television panel, which was broadcasting a cricket match, was framed in gold.

Reggie looked to be in his forties. A younger man sat in a leather chair in one corner of the room, preoccupied with his cell phone. I could see the strap of a shoulder holster peeking out from under the younger man's windbreaker. He looked innocent enough, but I suspected he knew enough to put the phone away in situations where he might need to pull his gun.

"Do you follow cricket?" Reggie asked, waving a gold ring-laden hand at the TV.

"No, I don't," I said.

"I was just flipping channels one day and found one that broadcasts cricket matches almost nonstop. I watched one, and man I was hooked," he said. "I still don't understand the rules completely, but it's a fascinating game to watch."

He gave me a few seconds to respond. I didn't.

"Okay," he said. "You said on the phone you had some kind of business opportunity you wanted to talk to me about."

I nodded toward the younger man with the phone and shrugged.

"Oh, that's just Curtis. He's okay."

"Fair enough," I said. "The business opportunity I mentioned is one that has come up recently on the west side of the State. Some guys I know had an interruption in their business operations and it has left us with an opening for the right person with the right kind of resources."

"Please, do tell me more," he said, raising the remote to mute the cricket play-by-play.

"It's pretty simple really," I said. "These guys had a transportation network set up that was paying off like a well-oiled machine until somebody came along and broke it. I'm here to try to put it back together again."

He smiled.

"I don't understand," he said. "Why would you come to me? I'm always looking for business opportunities, but what would my role be?"

"Well, that's pretty easy," I said. "Your role would be to unbreak what you broke."

"What?"

"Oh, come on," I said. "Benny Shanks was a friend of mine. He told me about you putting pressure on him to give you a taste of the money that was flowing to Benny from the setup. Benny wouldn't come across, so you took it upon yourself to interrupt the flow. Maybe you didn't intend to fully kill the goose that laid the golden egg, but that's how it turned out."

"I heard about Benny, and I am truly sorry that your friend was killed," he said. "But aside from that, I really don't know what you're talking about."

I shrugged.

"We've all gotta die someday," I said. "And, Benny lived to be an old man. Benny's gone now, but everything is still in place to put the pipeline back in operation if everybody can come to an understanding. And, I don't see why you couldn't be a full partner if you're willing to give back what you took. As sort of an initiation fee."

He was quiet for a few seconds, and then smiled.

"I would have to put some thought into that," he said.

I stood up.

"I'll be in touch," I said.

CHAPTER FIFTY-TWO
visitor

I rolled into Austin at sundown and telephoned a former partner after checking into a motel. We met for dinner at a place near the UT campus, and I got caught up on the latest interdepartmental politics and news about retirements and resignations of former officers we had both worked with. I found my energy level sagging after dinner and apologized for calling it an early night.

My motel room was quieter than the previous night, and I was so tired that I had no problem sleeping past sunrise, something I rarely did at home. I stopped by one of my favorite restaurants for breakfast and didn't get out of town and on the road until well into the morning.

When I got to Elmore, I decided to stop by the office and check the messages on the landline phone. As I parked on the street in front of Lita's and got out of my truck, Pete Rascon came out of the front entrance of the restaurant.

"Hey Buddy, I'm glad to see you back," he said, hurrying to meet me with a worried look on his face.

"Hey, Pete," I said. "Is everything okay?"

"I sure hope so. I just wanted to let you know that I let somebody into your office yesterday. I didn't know you wouldn't be back and he wanted to wait for you."

"Who was it?" I asked.

"Uh, I don't guess I know his name. It's that guy with the green hot rod car."

"Oh, Carter Branch?"

"I think so. Yeah, that sound right," he said. "I hope it was okay to let him in."

"Sure, Pete, no problem," I said, wondering why Carter Branch would have wanted Pete to give him access to my office.

When I got inside, I did a quick look around and didn't see anything out of the ordinary. The file folder containing the background information that Bob Clemmer had gathered on Carter Branch and Eli Trevisi and some notes I had made about Sandy Doyle's theory about Reggie Marshall being responsible for the truck hijackings was still on top of my desk where I'd left it.

Could a visitor left alone in my office have taken a look inside the folder?

Most certainly.

Would I have any way of knowing?

Nope.

I cursed myself for leaving the folder out in the open but knew that there was no way of knowing if the contents had been seen.

I locked up and drove home, deciding to swing by Mesa Guestsuites on the way. If Carter Branch had gained access to my office to snoop, why not confront him with the knowledge that I was aware he had been there?

Carter's car wasn't visible in the front parking lot, where I had seen it a couple of days earlier, so I parked and went inside.

The woman at the front desk was named 'Kasee' according to her employee badge, and she had silver balls protruding from piercings on both sides of the bridge of her nose.

"Hi," I said. "I wonder if you can help me. I've been out on a rig the last couple of days, but when I was leaving here the other morning I think I may have bumped the car that was parked next to me with my truck."

"Oh, no," she said. "Are you okay?"

"Oh, yeah, I'm fine. It was just a little bump, but the more I got to thinking about it the more I realized I should have tried to find out whose car it was and give them my insurance information."

"I see. Well, I don't think anybody has reported any damage to their vehicle, so maybe you didn't really hit it?"

She said the last part like it was a question, implying that maybe I should just skate free with no worries.

"Oh, I hit it alright," I said. "Spilled hot coffee all over myself when it happened. I really feel bad about leaving, and I even got the license number of the car, but I didn't want to go to the police or I might end up in jail for hit and run."

"That wouldn't be good," she said. "Especially when you're trying to do the right thing."

"I was hoping you might be able to tell me if whoever owns the car is still here. That way, I can give them my information."

She frowned and thought about it for a few seconds.

"Or, if you're not comfortable with that," I said. "I can leave my information with you and you can give it to them."

"I would really appreciate it," I said, sliding a piece of paper with the description of Carter Branch's car and license number 'TT4'.

She didn't answer but moved to her computer and hit a few keys.

"I'm sorry," she said, handing the piece of paper back. "It looks like they left last night. I really wish I could help you, but the security of our guests is a really big deal for us."

"That's okay," I said. "I understand."

CHAPTER FIFTY-THREE
search party

I had just gotten back in my pickup when the phone rang.

"Mr. Griffin?"

It was Granny Mo. She told me she had seen a man knocking on the door of Courtney Ramey's trailer and then trying to pry open one of the windows. She called the police and two cruisers had arrived and were holding the man while they investigated.

"Are the police still there?" I asked.

"Yes, they are. They've got the man in the back of their patrol car and they're talking to Courtney right now."

I drove to the Ramey's trailer expecting to find either Jimmy or Timmy in custody. I recognized one of the officers so I parked and waited for him to acknowledge me before approaching.

"Is everything okay?" I asked. "I've been trying to help Mrs. Ramey locate her missing husband."

"I'm not really sure what's going on here," he said. "She's scared to death that this guy was going to break in and do something, but she can't decide if she wants to press charges."

"What's his name?" I asked.

"No clue. He's not talking. But the tattoos on his face look like the ones we saw on an MS-13 member they arrested in Odessa for those murders last year."

The Salvadoran street gang named Mara Salvatrucha, and commonly called MS-13, was now international, but with hundreds of members believed to be operating in Texas. The Mexican drug cartels had been known to recruit MS-13 members for their especially brutal brand of violence.

I walked over to get a look at the man in the back of the unit. He was younger than I expected, but his heavily tattooed face, including the letters 'MS' on his forehead told me the officer was right.

"Have you explained why she needs to file charges?" I asked. "This guy would have killed her and her kids if he'd been able to get inside."

"We're talking that through with her," he said. "She was to scared to even talk when we first got here."

CHAPTER FIFTY-FOUR
justin dials in

Justin Ramey called me thirty minutes later. We talked for half an hour as he laid out what happened the night of the last welding truck run and where he'd been hiding out since. I'd been fairly accurate in my speculation about how things had gone down. Justin had driven one of the welding trucks to the yard in Van Horn, where the Mexican driver had been waiting with the other truck. Justin had known something was different about that night's meeting because the other driver normally showed up alone, but had another man with him this time, and the driver seemed nervous. After getting chased by men shooting at him from a car and trying to escape down an oilfield lease road that ended in a dead end, Justin had been able to get out of the welding truck and run away into the darkness of the sand dunes surrounding the graded pumpjack location. He said he must have lost his phone when he was making his getaway, but never considered going back to try to find it. Instead, he tried to get as far away from the sound of gunfire as he could, walking across the open country in a direction he hoped would lead him towards Elmore.

"But then I got to thinking about what might be in that truck," he said. "I knew it was something important. That's why Trey was so careful with the rules he gave me about not making any stops and not taking a phone with me and keeping things so confidential. I figured it was probably drugs, and probably enough to be worth a lot of money. And, I was the one who was responsible for getting the truck back to Andrews that night. I knew I'd be in trouble, so I wasn't sure what to do."

"Since I hadn't seen any of those guys run after me on foot, I decided to walk back to see if they'd left yet. Once I got close enough I could see they had like a big tow truck or something backed up to the back end of the welding truck and there was a guy crawling around under it and there were sparks coming from under the truck. He worked under there for a while and then they hooked a line to the back end of the welding truck and just lifted the back end of the bed up. A couple of guys started pulling these black bundles out of the back end of the welding truck and putting them in the trunk of the car that had been chasing me and into this SUV that had also shown up by then. I just kept watching while they let the back end of the welding bed back down and then set fire to the truck. Then they all drove off."

"I looked around for my phone for a little while but couldn't find it. So, I just started walking. I knew where the highway was from the headlights of cars going by, so I stayed off the road but close enough that I knew I wasn't walking in circles. I thought about trying to catch a ride but I was afraid those guys who were after me might still be looking for me, so I just kept on walking until I could see the lights of Kermit and then walked on into town. It was almost daylight by then so I found a little motel where I could get a room pretty cheap and checked in and crashed. I slept all that day and when I woke up I still didn't know what to do, so I just stayed in that room and watched TV. Trey had started paying me before I made each run just so I'd always have at least three hundred bucks on me in case there was mechanical trouble with one of the trucks and I needed money to get it back on the road. So, I had a little money, and I needed some time to think. I watched some movies and I would just walk down the street to the Pizza Hut or the barbecue place when I got hungry."

"How long did you stay there?" I asked.

"I think I paid for three nights, which counted the night I made the run, because they charged me for a night even though I didn't check in until it was almost morning."

"What did you do then?"

"Well, I knew I had to call somebody, and I knew Courtney would be worried to death about me by then. So, I called Benny first and told him the whole story. He said everybody was looking for me and were starting to say that maybe I took off with the dope and pointing fingers at him too since I'm his nephew. But, he said it would all be okay. He just needed some time to explain things to people."

"Which people?"

"He didn't say, and I knew it was

better if I didn't ask. He told me to stay put and he'd send somebody to get me. So, a guy picked me up a few hours later and drove me to an empty house in Hobbs that I guess Benny owns, and that's where I've been ever since."

"Are you there by yourself?"

"Yeah. The guy that picked me up just gave me the key to the place and left."

"You still got money left for food?"

"Yeah, but I need to come home. I miss Courtney and kids."

I told Justin I was trying to make it safe for him to return home and made him promise to stay where he was until I had done so. But, I didn't tell him that I still wasn't exactly clear on how I was going to do that.

CHAPTER FIFTY-FIVE
brain freeze report

"Well, I've got some news," Clemmer said, slapping a file folder down on the table and opening it.

I had been waiting for him at The Bagel Barn since shortly after he called and asked to meet.

"Not a good news, bad news deal? Just plain old news?" I said.

"Just plain old news," he said. "First, there were a couple of pretty good prints on the Texas Brain Freeze cup, and they came up as a match for a gang-banger from Houston named Donald 'D-Thang' Wilkins."

"Well, I'd say that qualifies as a good news item, wouldn't you?" I asked.

"Second, the gang unit at the Houston PD confirms that D-Thang is associated with Reggie Marshall's drug operation."

"Even better," I said.

"Third, D-Thang was shot and killed in a beef with a bouncer at a club in Houston three days after Benny Shanks was killed."

"Well, that's not good," I said. "The cup helps us establish that Reggie Marshall was there the night Benny was shot, but with D-Thang dead we can't go after him to put leverage on Reggie."

"Just have to find a different way," Clemmer said. "You'll come up with something."

CHAPTER FIFTY-SIX
keep it clean

It didn't take long for Reggie Marshall to make up his mind about the offer I made to him, and the little summit that I set up took place on a Monday afternoon a week later.

Monday afternoons were always slow at Lita's, and Pete Rascon was more than agreeable to providing a meeting room with very few questions asked. He cooperated fully when I introduced him to Shane Gerber, who called himself

Tom Whitworth, and explained that his tech guys needed access to the room a few days ahead of time to make sure things were set up for a financial planning seminar he would be conducting.

"Do you need it catered?" Pete asked.

Shane/Tom looked at me and I shrugged.

"Sure," Shane/Tom said. "Could you set up a little buffet at one end of the room with a few items on it? Nothing too elaborate. I don't want my guests eating a big meal and falling asleep during my presentation."

"I got you," Pete said. "We'll keep it simple."

"Oh, and one other thing," Shane/Tom said. "These people who are coming are all wealthy men who enjoy being served by attractive young women. Do you mind if I bring my own crew of servers for the event?"

"I got no problem with that," Pete said. "Long as everybody keeps their clothes on. This is a family establishment, you understand."

"Got it," Shane/Tom said.

CHAPTER FIFTY-SEVEN
the whole enchilada

Frank Delano was the first to arrive, accompanied by Tim Kettle, who probably still held a grudge for the footprints I had left on his pickup. As I had spelled out in the ground rules, each invitee was allowed to bring one other person, but nobody was supposed to be armed once they left their vehicles. Tim and any other sidekicks who showed up would need to wait in my office until the summit concluded and wouldn't be allowed to leave until everybody was ready to leave.

One of Shane Gerber's DEA agents, wearing a Mr. Robot T-shirt and preoccupied with the lines of code appearing on the screen of my PC, didn't even look up to acknowledge the presence of new people in the room.

"Computer problems," I said as we walked past. "This guy's supposed to be genius, but so far I'm not impressed."

I handed the TV remote to Tim and led Delano into the restaurant and down the hall to the meeting room. The three young women that Shane Gerber had brought along to act as servers were busy getting the buffet table ready as I showed Delano to the table.

"Nice setup," he said, leering at the women. "Never hurts to have a little eye candy around."

Sammy Rosado showed up next, quietly instructing his escort Gonzalo in Spanish to be ready for anything. Gonzalo, who could smell the aromas wafting through the air from the other part of the building responded by asking if they were going to eat while they were here. Sammy didn't respond, but after I got Sammy situated in the meeting room I found Pete Rascon and asked if he would put together a sampler platter of appetizers for the guys waiting in my office.

Trey Jenkins arrived alone and looking understandably nervous.

"Just follow my lead, and everything will be cool," I said quietly as we walked back to the meeting room.

Frank and Sammy already had plates full of food in front of them, and the servers were giggling and acting like a group of high school girls instead of the trained DEA agents they were.

I let everyone get settled and continue eating and flirting with the undercover servers while I waited for Reggie Marshall to arrive. The parties in place so far kept respectful distances from each other, sitting at least one chair apart from the next guy at the long rectangular table.

Finally, Frank Delano spoke up.

"Hey, I know this is your party, but don't you think you ought to get the show on the road? I got places I could be and things I could be doing."

"I'm just about to get things started," I said. "Give me just a second."

I walked back to my office to find Tim Kettle and Gonzalo both intently watching an infomercial for a collapsible garden hose from opposite sides of the room. A big black SUV pulled up outside and I watched as Reggie Marshall and his driver 'just Curtis' exited and came inside. We got Curtis settled, sulking in the corner and ignoring the other two members of the left-behind party, and then I took Reggie over to the meeting next door.

"Who the fuck's this you're bringing in here?" Delano said, as we sat down.

"Gentlemen, let me introduce Reggie Marshall," I said. "I'll explain why he's here in a few minutes."

"Before we get started, there is one more thing."

I pulled my cell phone from its holster on my hip.

"Let's all let the ladies hold our phones until this is over. I'd like to keep the interruptions to a minimum."

With that, one of the servers walked up and retrieved my phone, then waited as each of the attendees surrendered their phones. She exited the room with them, followed by the other two servers, who paused to close the door when they left.

"Okay, now to the reason we're here," I said. "Frank, Trey, Sammy, you guys had a good thing going with Benny. It was such a good thing that it would be a shame if you don't do everything you can to try to put it back together after the little hiccup you suffered."

"It was more than a little hiccup," Delano grumbled.

"I know, I know," I said. "And, I'm not saying it will be a small thing to try to overcome. People have taken hits and things need to be put right before things can get rolling again."

"Damn right people took hits. Somebody burned my house down and killed my dog," Trey said, right on cue.

"You're right, Trey, you took a hit," I said.

"I got people breathing down my neck for the money they lost," Delano said.

"Oh, cry me a river," Sammy Rosado said. "The people talking to me ain't just breathing down my neck, they're looking to put a machete through it."

"This is what I'm talking about," I said. "You can't just start back up until you make things right. You can't let resentments fester and come between you. So, you'll all need to talk some more about that."

"But, the reason I brought Reggie Marshall to this meeting is because he has assured me that he can help you get the missing money and meth back if he gets a piece of the action in the future."

"What's your involvement here?" Delano asked, looking at me. "Are you taking over Benny's spot?"

"No, I'm here because I owed Benny for helping me out in the past, and because I was hired to try to find Benny's nephew. Reggie here is the one who wants to take over Benny's spot."

"And, let me just say," Reggie said. "I intend to sweeten the deal for you all by providing additional connections so that you can easily double the amounts you were moving before."

"What makes you think you can get the money and meth back?" Delano asked.

"Because I'm the one who took it," Reggie calmly replied.

"What the hell?" Delano said.

"Not a smart move," Sammy said. "Not smart at all."

"Listen to him," I said. "Try to look past what happened before and focus on what's ahead."

"What's ahead is this guy ending up with a bullet in his head," Delano said. "The guys I answer to don't mess around."

"You can all put this back together," I said. "But, Reggie's return of the money and meth is just a part of it. There should be reparations for those who were wronged. That's the other reason I'm here."

"Trey here lost a house worth half a million dollars," I said. "So, Frank, that's on you since it was your guys who burned it down."

Delano gave an almost

imperceptible nod.

"We're going to need at least two more welding trucks to get started," I said. "More once Reggie gets some additional connections for us. Sammy, that's on your end. You're all going to all have to put money in equally to build the trucks though."

"There's one more thing," I said, turning to Reggie. "The driver of that welding truck your guys chased down is still missing. He's the nephew of Bennie Shanks and I need this resolved before it will be safe for you to start back up. A hundred grand to his wife should take care of it, and it should come from you since your guys are responsible for whatever happened to him."

"And, Benny Shanks widow needs half a million for Benny's life," I said. "That's on you too, since you had him killed."

"Christ, you killed Benny?" Delano said, looking at Reggie. "Why?"

"He wouldn't listen to reason," said Reggie. "It wasn't nothing personal. Just business. He didn't want me as a partner. Said he wouldn't even present it to the rest of you. I told him I was going to be part of this one way or another. He was the one who chose how it all worked out. So, here I am."

"Oh, and Reggie," I said. "I need you to deliver thirty-five thousand dollars in cash to Sandy Doyle tomorrow morning. Just tell him it's from me. He'll be expecting it."

"Sandy Doyle? What the hell is that for?" Reggie asked.

"Just call it my finder's fee," I said..

CHAPTER FIFTY-EIGHT
stung

I excused myself from the summit, telling them they could work out the rest of the details without me, and returned to my office where I waited for things to be wrapped up.

A few minutes later, the attendees began streaming through, Sammy Rosado carrying a to-go box for Gonzalo, and Frank Delano pausing just inside the restaurant to make sure one of the young DEA agent/servers he had been eyeing had his personal contact information.

Once everybody was gone, I went back to the meeting room where I found Shane Gerber and the other agents seated around the table. They appeared to be conducting an informal post mortem meeting. I stepped back into the hallway and waited for Shane to appear.

"How did we do?" I asked.

"Couldn't have gone any better," Shane said. "The sound was good and the camera placement was perfect. Plus, we were able to get some useful information off their phones while we were holding them."

"Like we talked about the other day," he said. "The current strategy within the Department is more focused on waiting, watching, and building cases to see where they lead rather than on making one-time busts. So, I can't promise you that we'll take these guys down right away if they follow through on the plan you laid out for them. We'll want to follow the chain both directions, as far as we can, and build airtight cases before we spring our trap."

"Did you talk to Clemmer?" he asked.

"I did," I said. "He understands the game plan and knows that it would be better to hit Reggie with conspiracy to commit murder in combination with trafficking, whenever you're ready to do that."

"Good," he said. "We want to maximize the payoff on this operation. If it works out right, everybody involved in this will be in jail eventually. As long as Trey Jenkins continues to cooperate he should come out okay, relatively speaking."

"I think he'll continue to give you whatever he can," I said.

"This Frank Delano guy hasn't even been on our radar before," he said. "So, we'll be able to follow what goes on at his place and see where that leads."

I told him the story that Carter Branch had related about the repackaging of the dope inside insulation panels. But, also told him that Bob Clemmer hadn't been able to substantiate the story about the truck driver keeling over in a diner in Rolla, Missouri."

"So, this Eli Trevisi might be a player in this too?" he said, jotting down the name.

"Anything's possible," I said. "Carter Branch seemed like a pretty straight shooter, but he's also got a CIA background, so when he told me the story it sounded legitimate. But, when I found out later that Eli and Benny have been good friends for years, Carter's story didn't make any sense."

"Unless, Benny figured out a way to get those insulation panels transported on one of Eli's trucks without Eli himself knowing," he offered.

"We may never know the answer to that one," I said.

CHAPTER FIFTY-NINE
paid in full

Two days later, I answered my phone to hear the unmistakable rasp of Sandy Doyle's voice.

"Your boy's off the hook," he said. "One of Reggie Marshall's runners brought the cash in yesterday. I'm glad this ain't one more debt I've got to write off, but honestly it kind of breaks my heart to see it cleared up so quickly. I never even got a chance to talk to the good Sheriff in person."

"It would be best for everyone if

you kept it that way," I said.

"Shame. I coulda built him into a lifelong customer. Tell me, who got into bed with Reggie Marshall? You? Or, the Sheriff."

"Neither," I said. "It's complicated. But, I appreciate you pointing me in Reggie's direction. I have a feeling that things will probably work out to your satisfaction when it's all over."

"Huh," he said. "But it's never really over, is it? Never mind the fat lady singing and all that."

"You're right about that, Sandy. It just keeps going on, and on, and on. See you around."

"Yeah. See you around."

CHAPTER SIXTY
cruller

"You know, this is not a proper cruller, even though everybody calls it that."

Norris Jackson went on for several minutes explaining the history of the traditional cruller pastry and its evolution into the product sold by donut shops.

Norris had dropped by the morning after I called to tell him his debt with Sandy Doyle had been cleared up. I didn't mention that it was done using money extracted from Reggie Marshall. I figured the knowledge could only taint any determination Norris might have to make a new start and leave gambling behind for good.

"How the heck did that happen?" he asked.

"Long story," I said. "But, it's done, so don't worry about it."

He went on for several minutes over the phone about how grateful he was, and how he had learned his lesson and had been attending Gamblers Anonymous meetings regularly. He was also adamant that he would repay me every penny. His repayment of the money was an important part of atoning for what he had done, but I didn't tell him that any amounts he repaid to me would be contributed in kind to a local charitable foundation that doled out funds to several local non-profit groups.

His dropping by with a box of donuts was an extension of his gratitude, but neither of us brought up the debt or the gambling again that day.

When he ran out of stories about the history of crullers, I opened the desk drawer.

"Let me show you something," I said. I pulled the white plastic jewelry store bag out of the drawer and reached inside to pull out the ring box. I sat it down on the desk and opened it.

"Wow," he said. "I don't know what to say."

He picked up the ring box for a closer look, and then looked at me solemnly.

"This is really beautiful, but you do understand I'm already married, don't you?"

CHAPTER SIXTY-ONE
ski masks

About a week later, Shane Gerber walked in and sat down in front of my desk, shaking his head.

"Weird how this stuff happens," he said. "I don't get over this way very often, and I almost never drive through Elmore, but I was driving through here today when I got this call from a contact in Houston."

"This morning," he continued. "Three guys wearing ski masks and carrying semi-autos busted into

Reggie Marshall's office, shot it out with Reggie's crew, and ended up killing three of them. The receptionist was lucky enough to come in late this morning and found the place shot up when she got there."

"What about Reggie?" I asked.

"He was there. The security video shows one of the three guys slapping him around and then dragging him out the front door."

"That could throw a wrench in your investigation," I said.

"Yeah, odds are Reggie may not make it out of this alive," he said. "Have to wait and see."

He stood up to go.

"Oh, and before I forget," he said. "I did some checking on Eli Trevisi. Our Kansas City office was familiar with him, but not as a player in any investigations. He's a big supporter of a local drug rehab program they have up there and is a personal friend of the head of the DEA field office. Apparently one of Eli's brothers got pretty heavily into drugs and died as a result. This was years ago."

The fact that Eli had lost a brother to drug abuse might help explain why he was reluctant to go in partners with Benny Shanks on the meth transport operation. But, I still had some unanswered questions about the involvement of Eli's trucks in the operation, or whether there even was any such involvement.

Shane gave me a follow-up call a few days later about the discovery of Reggie Marshall's body.

"They found him inside Mexico, hanging from a bridge near Juarez," he said. "He was missing his hands."

I guess I should have felt some

responsibility for Reggie Marshall's gruesome death, but I kept seeing the crime scene photos from Benny's murder and thinking about how close Justin Ramey had come to losing his life. And, how nonchalantly Reggie had responded when asked why he killed Benny. Live by the sword, die by the sword.

CHAPTER SIXTY-TWO
place holder

"No, I don't need to," Angie said, holding the ring up to the light. "It fits perfectly, and I think it's beautiful."

"I know it's beautiful," I said. "But the woman at the jewelry store said it would be no problem to bring it back and get something you like better. And, we figured you'd need to get it resized anyway. I just needed a place-holder to use when I popped the question."

"Do you like it?" she asked, holding it up and displaying it like it was a prize on a game show.

"Sure, I do," I said.

"Then, it's good enough for me. Now, on to more important stuff. Like, when are we going to do this and where are we going to go afterwards?"

"I think that will depend on your schedule," I said. "I don't have a lot on my plate now that Justin Ramey is back with his family and everybody involved in Benny Shanks murder is dead."

"So, you don't have to worry about testifying anytime soon as far as Shane Gerber's investigation into the meth trafficking."

"No, Reggie Marshall was killed before he could return the money and drugs, so as far as Shane can tell, the meth pipeline that Benny, Trey and Sammy set up is still shut down."

"Maybe we should start making a list," she said.

"A list of what?" I said.

"Of places we can go on our honeymoon, silly."

"Oh, okay. Let me get a pen."

CHAPTER SIXTY-THREE
Eli

Work slowed down for me with the news of Reggie Marshall's death, which wasn't necessarily a bad thing since discussions of wedding and honeymoon plans began to occupy more of my time.

Bob Clemmer was relieved to have the books on the Benny Shanks murder closed without the mountain of paperwork and follow-up that accompanied most closed cases. He had offered to bring me in on some other cases he was working, and I planned to take him up on it, but decided I needed to concentrate my attentions on Angie at the moment.

So far, we had made pretty firm decisions that we would have a small, informal ceremony at the home of one of Angie's friends, and that we would live in Angie's house after the wedding. It was slightly smaller than my parents' house, but at least twenty-five years newer. It was a good time to put my parents' place on the market, with real estate in Elmore selling at a premium due to the number of oilfield workers being brought to town by the busy oilfield.

We still didn't have any honeymoon plans made, and neither of us had any destination calling out to us.

"I just want to go somewhere we can relax," she would say. "Some place we can do nothing all day if we feel like it."

I was sitting in my office on a Tuesday afternoon, clicking through a travel review website, when Carter Branch walked in, followed by a slightly older gentleman that he introduced as Eli Trevisi.

Carter explained that they had flown into Midland International on Eli's private jet and had gone by to visit Maria Schankowitz.

"She's a strong woman, and she'll be fine," Eli said. "But, I just needed to pay my respects in person and make sure she knows that the bond I had with Benny continues with her."

"And, I wanted to stop by to personally thank you," he continued, as we sat down around my desk. "For what you did to find out who killed Benny. Carter told me all about it."

"I was just following up on what other people told me," I said. "I wish we could have brought the people responsible to justice."

"Oh, they got their justice," he said. "Sometimes these things just have a way of working themselves out."

The way he said that last bit made me wonder if Eli might have had a hand in making sure things worked out the way they had for Reggie.

Eli was curious to know more about the oil industry, so we talked about that a while, and then about the trucking business, and then about Lake of the Ozarks, where Carter Branch's business was located, and where Eli kept a vacation home.

"You've never seen the lake?" he asked incredulously. "Oh, my God, you've got to come spend some vacation time up there. I've got a house right on the water that I never use. Carter takes care of the place, but you could come up there and stay as long as you like. You've got to. I insist. As a way of repaying you for all you did for Benny and Maria."

"I'll promise to think about it," I said.

CHAPTER SIXTY-FOUR
lake life

"I could get used to this," Angie said, for the third time that afternoon.

"You said that already," I told her.

"I just want you to know how much I meant it the first time," she said.

We were sitting on a verandah facing the water at Eli Trevisi's 12,000 square-foot vacation home on Lake of the Ozarks. There were three such verandahs on the property, but this one was off of the bedroom we were using while spending the week relaxing and exploring the area.

I had presented Eli's offer of his vacation home to Angie as a possible honeymoon destination and after looking at pictures of the area online she quickly moved it to the top of the list.

The musical chime of the doorbell signaled Carter Branch's arrival. He was accompanied by an attractive young woman that he introduced as Kinley Walters.

"Kinley works for me," he said, as we stood in the foyer doing introductions. "She keeps my schedule straight and explains to people why I can't be in two places at the same time."

"Some of these absentee owners get a little frantic if they think things might not be perfect when they arrive for their weekend," she said. "Carter has spoiled them over the years, and now they don't understand that he has more than one client to take care of."

"It sounds like a fascinating business," Angie said. "I bet it gets busy when the weather turns this nice and everybody wants to come to the lake."

"It gets a little crazy," Carter said. "I wish I could clone myself when this time of year rolls around."

"So, are you guys up for a boat ride?" Kinley asked.

"If you're sure you don't mind showing us around," I said.

"Oh, no, we love an excuse to take Eli's boat out," Carter said. "You won't believe how nice it is."

Kinley and Angie went off to the kitchen to finish packing up the hors d'oeuvres Angie and I had been working on earlier.

I followed Carter outside and

down to the dock, where we did some last-minute preparations on the boat. Eli had three boats he kept at Lake of the Ozarks. Two of them were kept at the dock in front of the lake house. One of those was a typical 20-foot bass boat, with the flat platform deck, trolling motor mounted on the front, and padded elevated seats at the front and rear for fishing. The other was a gleaming new 46-foot express cruiser, with a cabin below that looked like the inside of a luxury motor home. This would be our boat for the day.

The third boat was a 52-foot high performance racing boat sponsored by Trevisi Transport and maintained at a nearby marina by the team that raced it. According to Carter, although Eli had done some boat racing himself in his younger days, he rarely piloted the

52-footer himself.

"Let me ask you something straight up," I said, as Carter showed me around the boat. "That story you told me about Eli finding drugs hidden in the insulation panels his truck was hauling. You completely made that up, didn't you?"

He smiled.

"It sounded pretty good though, didn't it?" he said, with a laugh.

"Oh, I bought into it hook, line and sinker for a while," I said. "But, you know what ruined it? The truck driver's heart attack while eating supper."

"A little dramatic?" he said.

"A little," I said. "Plus, it wasn't hard to uncover the fact that Eli and Benny were close friends. Good story though. Inventive."

"It's a long drive from Lake of the Ozarks to Elmore, Texas," he said.

"I had a lot of time to think up a scenario. Eli knew what Benny was into and knew a little bit about how they were moving the dope, and who a few of the players were. Benny came to Eli to ask him if he wanted in when they were starting up, but Eli didn't want any part of it. He had a brother that OD'd when Eli was a teenager, so he wouldn't even consider getting involved in something like what Benny was doing."

"Then, why did you really go down to Elmore?"

"To find out who killed Benny," he said. "Benny's murder hit Eli hard, and he wanted to do something about it. See, Benny saved Eli's life in prison, and Eli felt like he owed a debt to Benny he could never pay back. He sent me down there to look into it while he tried reaching out to a few people in

Mexico."

"People in the drug cartels?" I asked.

"I'm not sure," he said. "Eli's made a lot of business connections in Mexico since NAFTA changed the way stuff can move by truck over the border."

Kinley and Angie came walking down the ramp to the dock rolling a wagon that contained enough food and refreshments to last us several days.

We spent the next several hours on a leisurely ride that followed the serpentine shape of the lake from Eli's house several miles into a less populated area situated within the borders of a state park. Carter piloted the boat into an uninhabited cove where we anchored while we ate, drank and swam in the lake until late afternoon. We packed up and started back up the lake towards Eli's place as the sun dipped lower and the angle of the light on the other boats made them take on a golden glow as they raced towards their homes or took up positions to watch the coming sunset.

Carter slowed the boat and dropped anchor just outside of Eli's cove so we wouldn't have far to travel once dusk overtook us. I pulled Angie close to me on the back deck of the boat and we enjoyed another sunset together. Although I hoped there would be many more sunsets like this one to come, I looked off toward the horizon and was humbled by an overpowering feeling of deep gratitude for what I had at that very moment.

If you enjoyed TWICE THE HEIST, be sure to read the first Buddy Griffin book:

TWO BITS FOUR BITS

Available on Amazon

ABOUT THE AUTHOR

Mark Cotton was born in Texas and grew up in southeastern New Mexico in the middle of the Permian Basin, one of the richest oil-producing regions in the country. With a background in business, he enjoys constructing stories with interesting characters and complex plot twists.

When he's not writing, Mark enjoys researching and documenting local history and traveling.

CPSIA information can be obtained
at www.ICGtesting.com
Printed in the USA
BVHW042205050820
585661BV00015B/292

9 781723 483035